RANGER BELIEF

TEXAS RANGER HEROES

LYNN SHANNON

RANGER BELIEF

There is no fear in love.

1 John 4:18

ONE

Someone was hunting in her woods.

Delaney "Laney" Torres bent next to the decaying corpse of a raccoon. It'd been shot in center mass, a clean kill that spoke of experience. Anger flared in her chest. This area of Piney Woods State Park was remote, but hunting of any kind was illegal. It was also dangerous. A stray shot could hit an innocent person. Hiking trails crisscrossed this entire area.

Scout whined softly beside her, the Labrador's ears pricked forward with concern. Laney stroked her partner's golden coat, grateful for the company even on routine patrol duties like this. "I know, girl. We'll figure out who did this." She used her flashlight to search the immediate area for any clues about the hunter. The grass near the road was tamped down, indicating a vehicle had been here recently, but the ground was too dry for tire impressions.

Her radio crackled. "Superintendent Torres, come in."

Surprise rippled through her. It was well after nine, and the visitor's center should be closed, the rangers on shift already at home, including her second-in-command, Andy Dawson. She pressed the button on the receiver attached to her shoulder. "I'm here, Andy."

"We got a call about fireworks in Campsite 8 from a concerned camper."

Fireworks were a problem this time of year. Summer had left a drought that brief September rains hadn't yet abated. The ground was covered with dry pine needles. Any spark could destroy the entire park and spread to the closest town, twenty miles away. There was a statewide ban on fireworks, and they were expressly forbidden inside Piney Woods, but that didn't stop everyone. Laney had confiscated more than her fair share this summer. Twelve hours into her shift, exhaustion pulled at her limbs, but she appreciated the concerned camper who'd called in the report.

"Thanks for letting me know. I'll check it out." She paused, then pressed the button on the receiver again. "Go home, Andy. The paperwork can wait until tomorrow."

"Finishing up this report and heading out, ma'am."

Andy's voice was weary, and Laney felt it down to her bones. With their superintendent on medical leave for cancer treatment and chronic staff shortages, everyone at Piney Woods was pulling double duty. As acting superintendent, she believed in leading by example and taking care of her staff, principles drilled into her during her Army days as a military police officer.

"Good. Make sure you forward the calls coming into the visitor center to the answering service." If there was an emergency, the answering service would call Laney. Any other issues would be dealt with in the morning. "Night, Andy."

"Good night, ma'am."

Laney swept her flashlight over the dead raccoon one more time. Judging from the bug activity, the kill was recent. Within the last couple of hours. Fresh anger swelled, but she forced herself to take a breath. Getting worked up wouldn't help the situation. The hunter had shot the poor animal for sport, which made it worse, but she'd deal with it. She made a mental note to address the issue with her staff in the morning. Patrolling rangers needed to remind campers that hunting in the park was illegal.

"Come on, Scout." Laney crossed to her SUV and opened the rear door. Scout hopped into her compartment. The Labrador had been her search-and-rescue partner for three years, trained to find missing campers and hikers in the vast park terrain. During her military days, Laney had worked with SAR dogs, so when the opportunity came to partner with Scout, she'd jumped at the chance. "We'll check out this fireworks complaint and then head home ourselves for some shut-eye. Maybe I'll even let you have the good treats tonight."

Scout's tail wagged, and Laney grinned. At least someone was having a good day.

She hopped in the driver's seat. The blast of cold air from the vent was refreshing. Darkness loomed ahead, trees and clouds swallowing the moonlight, leaving only her headlight beams to illuminate the narrow road as she headed for Campsite 8.

Her cell phone beeped with an incoming message that appeared on the screen embedded in her dash. A smile lifted the corners of her mouth when she saw it was from Jonah Foster, her best friend.

This was a terrible idea. Ryan is trying to set me up with his cousin from Dallas. I've been here 20 minutes and I'm already planning my escape route.

Laney chuckled. She'd intended to go to their mutual friend's birthday party, but when a park ranger called in sick, she'd taken the shift. Jonah had nearly bailed out of the event too, but she'd encouraged him to go. The man needed help in the socializing department. His work as a Texas Ranger kept him incredibly busy. If he didn't get out once in a while, he'd start growing roots to his desk.

She used voice activation to reply. "Don't be dramatic, Foster. It's a party. Mingle. And stop scowling—you're scaring people."

Her phone beeped a second later.

There's a guy here wearing a fringe vest and boots that have never seen dirt. I think I'm having an allergic reaction to the whole scene. Send backup. Or a medical excuse.

She rolled her eyes even as a familiar warmth spread through her chest. Laney could picture Jonah's expression perfectly, the barely there glower that made other people think he was intimidating, but she found endearing. Fifteen years of friendship had taught her to read all his micro-expressions. And honestly? She secretly loved that he texted her from parties he didn't want to be at.

She was about to reply when the wooden sign marking the footpath to Campsite 8 appeared. A late-model sedan was tucked among the trees just off the road. Laney pulled over, parking behind it, the mirth from her exchange with Jonah fading as she slipped on a professional mask. Scout picked up her head.

"Go back to sleep, girl. I'll be back in a jiffy."

Scout had developed a sensitivity to loud noises during her working years, so Laney left her behind when investigating fireworks complaints. The dog could handle most situations, but why stress her unnecessarily? She'd be better off in the car. The SUV was outfitted with a specialized idle system that kept the engine running and the air conditioning on but locked the vehicle down so no one could steal it without a key. A heat alarm would trigger if the A/C failed and the interior temperature rose even five degrees. She'd tested it herself last week.

Humidity hung heavy in the air as she flipped on her flashlight. The beam cut through the darkness, illuminating the footpath through the trees. An owl hooted overhead. Moonlight coated the leaves in a silvery glow, and despite the late hour and the long shift, she felt a familiar spark of gratitude. This was her favorite part of the job. Being out here under the stars, protecting this beautiful place. Her mom used to say that God painted the night sky just as carefully as He painted the dawn.

Looking at the silver-edged leaves and hearing the rustle of nocturnal life in the undergrowth, Laney believed it.

Campsite 8 was secluded and only used during the hot summer months by camping enthusiasts seeking a quiet escape near the lake. According to state park records, it'd been rented by a pair of college students for the weekend. Laney smiled. She remembered camping along this very lake with her own parents, back when things were simpler. Those were the happy memories. Before... well, before everything fell apart.

The trees parted, and Campsite 8 came into view. Flames glimmered in the firepit, popular rock music emanated from a speaker next to a set of camping chairs, and a large tent connected to a generator came into view. The ground was free of the little bits of paper left behind after exploding fireworks. Still, a whisper of apprehension crept down Laney's spine. She paused, uncertain about what had set off her internal warning system.

Where were the campers?

"Park Ranger. Anyone here?" Her gaze swept over the chairs and firepit, noting the package of graham crackers and chocolate. A half-cooked marshmallow on a prong rested in the dirt as if it'd been dropped. Drinks sat in cup holders in each of the chairs.

Maybe they'd gone for a late-night swim? The lake was beautiful this time of night, and young couples did spontaneous things. But even as the thought crossed her mind, unease tightened in her chest. The marshmallow in the dirt. The drinks sitting there. Something felt... off.

Strange. She drew closer, her light sweeping over the

campsite. The tent was big enough for two people and had a portable fan run by a generator. Two trash bags hung from a nearby tree, and a drinks cooler secured by a bungee cord rested on the picnic table. Other than the food discarded on the ground, the area was pristine. Judging from the tent setup and the care taken in handling the food and trash, the campers were experienced.

Laney bent and turned off the speaker. "Hello! Park Ranger!"

Technically, she was acting superintendent, but most civilians wouldn't know what that meant. Park ranger was universal.

Hair rose on the back of her neck as the sensation of being watched crept over her. She turned, her light cutting across the still waters of the lake and nearby bushes. Her heart thundered against her rib cage.

Nothing stirred. Still, the unease that plagued her from the moment she entered the campsite didn't abate. Her hand dropped to the holstered weapon at her hip, but she didn't draw it. "My name is Park Ranger Torres. Show yourself."

Silence followed. Laney drew in a breath. The humid air was thick, like soup, and scented with the heady smell of pine. Uncertainty warred with training. She'd always been thorough—some called it perfectionism—and her military training reinforced the importance of assessing threats carefully. But right now, she couldn't tell if her unease was justified or if she was being overly cautious.

Lord, help me know the difference between fear and

wisdom, she prayed silently, the familiar words bringing a measure of calm to her racing heart.

But she could rely on the facts. The campers weren't responding. They could be injured or in trouble. Either way, she needed to find them.

She turned and stepped closer to the tent.

That's when she smelled it.

The coppery scent of blood.

Her heart skipped a beat even as her fingers undid the button securing her weapon in its holster. She rounded the side of the tent, her flashlight beam illuminating the horrific sight in front of her. A young man lay face down on the ground. Dark blotches stained his T-shirt. Stabbed? Shot? She couldn't tell. His eyes were open and unseeing. She'd seen enough death to know. He was gone.

Where was the other camper? Laney vaguely remembered seeing him with a young woman when they checked in at the main lodge this morning. She yanked her weapon from its holster and swept her flashlight beam over the woods behind the tent.

A twig snapped. She whirled toward the sound, but a dark shadow exploded from the undergrowth, tackling her before she could react. She cried out as her gun was flung from her hand, landing in the dirt beyond her reach. Pain exploded through her body as she collided with the hard ground, the breath driven from her lungs as her attacker's weight slammed down on top of her. She struck him with the flashlight. He howled in rage.

A fist connected with her temple, sending stars

dancing across her vision. Before she could recover, strong hands encircled her throat. They were slick—gloves, maybe—and the scent of aftershave cut through the pine and blood. Something familiar about it tugged at her memory, but panic scattered the thought.

Her pulse hammered. The man straddled her, his weight trapping her arms against her sides. He was a dark blotch against the night. She tried to use her legs in a defensive move to wrap around his torso and throw him, but the angle was all wrong and his grip was too strong.

The pressure on her throat tightened. Darkness crept in at the edges of her vision. Panic took hold. She wriggled in a desperate attempt to get one hand free. Her lungs burned. She was seconds from losing consciousness when she felt the hard plastic of her SUV's key fob digging into her hip.

Scout! The dog was trained in search and rescue, but she'd also been trained to defend her handler. With blackness threatening to take over completely, her fingers fumbled desperately with the fob. Just as her vision began to tunnel, she found the button that would automatically open the rear door of the SUV, releasing Scout from her crate.

The sound of barking erupted through the night, fierce and protective.

It was the last thing she heard before the darkness claimed her.

TWO

Something felt... off.

Jonah Foster checked his phone again. An hour had passed since his last text to Laney, and she still hadn't responded. That wasn't like her, especially when her shift was winding down. He'd taken photos of the celebration and sent them to her, along with one of him looking miserable. They were designed to get a snarky reaction, but she hadn't replied.

He leaned back in the booth. Ingrained habit had him scanning the room. Half-eaten cake slices littered the sticky table. Country music blared from the speakers set up near the bar, and couples whirled on the dance floor. In another ten minutes, he could leave without being rude. Part of him felt guilty for bailing on Ryan and Catherine's party early. He liked them, but the honky-tonk scene wasn't for him. The drinking, the loud music, and the crowds gave him social anxiety.

He'd only come to the event in the first place because

Laney talked him into it. They hadn't seen each other in weeks, a byproduct of hectic schedules. He'd just closed a weeks-long investigation into a mall shooting, and she'd been pulling extra shifts. Summer was high season at the state park, and with Laney becoming the acting superintendent, her workload had doubled.

Jonah missed her.

Denise, Ryan's younger sister, weaved through the crowd to the table. Her cheeks were flushed from dancing, and her eyes bright with happiness. The pretty blonde had been flirting with Jonah for most of the evening, and he braced himself to make polite conversation.

"Hey!" Denise waved a hand in front of her face as she collapsed into the booth next to Jonah. "I haven't danced this much in ages." She picked up her half-drunk beer from the table and took a long sip before smiling broadly at him. "It's nice of you to guard our drinks, but I feel bad leaving you here alone."

"I don't mind." It was better to sit at the table than embarrass himself on the dance floor. God had given him many talents, but Jonah had been absent the day He'd handed out rhythm.

Denise set her beer back down on the table. "Ryan mentioned you're in law enforcement."

She had to shout to be heard over the loud music. Jonah nodded in reply. Yelling his job title in a crowded bar was reckless, and getting closer to Denise felt awkward.

She tilted her head coltishly. "I can see it. You've got

that dark and brooding look about you." Denise scooted closer and placed a hand on his arm. "I'm sure the job is stressful. All the more reason to kick back and have some fun when you're off duty. Come on, just one dance?"

An internal war raged within Jonah. He should tell her yes. Denise was gorgeous and fun-loving, a third-grade teacher living in Amarillo with a pet cat named Boots. She was exactly the kind of woman he should be pursuing. Except there was one small problem. The spark was missing. In his younger years, he might've forced himself to give it a chance, see where things went. Now, he was old enough to recognize that he just wasn't interested.

He needed to come up with a gentle excuse for bowing out of her request. And fast. His mind went blank—why was declining a dance so much harder than interrogating suspects?

Jonah's cell phone vibrated, Laney's name lighting up the screen. Relief washed through him as he scooped up the phone. "Sorry, Denise. I have to take this." He slid from the booth and hit answer, hurrying across the bar in search of a quiet spot. "Laney, you're gonna owe me big time for bailing on this event, just so you know." He ducked into the hall leading to the bathroom, and the noise dropped by several decibels. "Do you hear the music? It's enough to give anyone—"

"Jonah." Her voice was a rasp, raw and painful-sounding.

He stiffened. "What's wrong? Are you okay?"

"I'm fine." A pause. "Mostly. I need you to come to

the park to help with an investigation. A murder case." Her voice was rough and yet somehow also strangely hollow, with an underlying tremor that made his blood run cold. The only time Jonah had ever heard Laney like that was when her mother passed away. "It's... complicated. I'll explain everything when you get here. Campsite 8."

It was highly unusual for the park rangers to ask for assistance on a murder case from the Texas Rangers. Normally, the sheriff's department would step in. Whatever had happened was bad. Her voice told him she was barely holding it together. He calculated how long it would take him to drive to Piney Woods with his lights and sirens on. His truck was unmarked but equipped with all the official equipment necessary for a law enforcement officer.

Heat and humidity smacked him in the face as he exited the honky-tonk. "I'll be there in thirty minutes."

"Don't drive recklessly. The scene isn't going anywhere."

It was just like Laney to be in the middle of a crisis but still worry about him. Jonah scowled as he hopped into his truck and fired up the engine. "You're not the boss of me, Torres. I'll drive as fast as I want to."

The response got him the chuckle he'd hoped for, and some of the knots twisting his insides loosened. He wanted to ask if Laney was okay, but that was a silly question. She obviously wasn't. So he'd get to her as fast as he could. "See you soon."

His heart clenched when she said goodbye. Jonah

switched on his lights and siren before speeding out of the parking lot toward the highway.

His best friend needed him.

And he couldn't get to her fast enough.

THREE

Jonah made it to Piney Woods State Park in twenty-eight minutes. It took another ten to navigate the narrow two-lane road to Campsite 8. The sheer number of law enforcement vehicles in the area deepened his worry. He took in the crime scene tape, the clump of deputies gathered around another patrol car, and a set of paramedics loading a stretcher into the back of a bus.

No sign of Laney.

The park ranger manning the main entrance had radioed his arrival, so she knew Jonah was on site. He tucked his truck behind a patrol car, killed the engine, and unlocked the safe hidden under the passenger seat before removing his holstered weapon and ranger badge. It took precious seconds to don them, along with his sports coat and cowboy hat, but it was necessary to do so. Part of his job as a Texas Ranger was presenting a professional appearance even if every nerve in his body urged him to find Laney ASAP.

His boots tamped down the grass as he exited his vehicle. Jonah headed for a nearby deputy to ask about Laney when she appeared on a small footpath, Scout at her side. His heart skipped several beats as he took in her mussed uniform and carefully controlled expression. Without hesitation, Jonah ducked under the crime scene tape, intent on closing the distance between them, when a rough hand clamped down on his arm.

"Sir, you need to get behind the yellow line." The deputy's tone brooked no argument. His scowl was fierce, and his grip firm.

"Texas Ranger Jonah Foster." He shifted his sports coat to reveal the badge pinned to his chest. "Stand down, deputy. I've been called in to assist on this investigation."

The deputy's gaze flickered to Jonah's badge, but his expression didn't lose an ounce of suspicion, nor did he release him. "By whom?"

"He's with me, Harry." Laney's voice came from behind Jonah, and the roughness in it tightened his muscles. He shook off the deputy's restricting grip and turned to face her.

His breath stalled. Dirt and grass stained her rumpled uniform, and her normally neat hair was mussed and twisted into a bun. A pine needle was still tangled in the strands. Her messy appearance and stoic countenance would have been enough to raise concern, but it was the bruises around her neck that hit him like a physical blow. Dark fingermarks that made his stomach clench with fury.

Someone had tried to strangle her.

When his gaze caught hers, a myriad of emotions flickered in the depths of those gorgeous deep brown eyes. Relief. Worry. And buried deep... fear.

Jonah closed the distance between them in two strides. The urge to hug her, to comfort and protect her, was overwhelming, and somehow, she sensed it. Laney put up a hand to ward him off. "I'm fine." She bit her lip and whispered, "Please don't. I'll fall apart."

He drew up short, forcing himself to hold back. For her sake. "What happened?"

"I stumbled onto the scene of a double murder, and the killer attacked me." Laney reached down to pet Scout. The dog leaned her body against Laney's, clearly attuned to her handler's distress. "Scout came to my rescue. She chased the perpetrator away seconds before I passed out."

But Jonah heard the barest tremble in her words and caught the way her fingers shook as she stroked Scout's golden fur. A whirlwind of emotions twisted his insides like a hurricane. Anger that someone had laid hands on her, horror at the brutal nature of the attack, worry for her well-being, and a deep need to comfort her. Over-laying all of that was the realization that while he'd been griping about attending a friend's birthday party, she'd been in a fight for her life.

He'd nearly lost her.

It was a terrifying thought, one that could cripple him if he let it. So Jonah shoved all of those fears, worries, and thoughts aside. Laney needed his skills as a Texas Ranger.

The rest... they'd deal with that later.

"Walk me through what happened," Jonah said.

She straightened, chin lifting. "At 9:15, the main lodge received a call from a concerned camper who reported hearing fireworks coming from Campsite 8. I was doing a final patrol with Scout and was alerted to the complaint at 9:16. I arrived at the campsite fifteen minutes later, at 9:29." She gestured to her truck, buried behind a wall of patrol cars and the coroner's van. "I parked there. Scout stayed in the vehicle."

Jonah knew the golden Labrador had a sensitivity to loud noises, especially anything that resembled gunfire or flashbangs, so it wasn't surprising Laney left her behind. He followed his best friend onto the footpath, carefully stepping where she did along a predetermined route. Forensic technicians would comb the entire area for evidence.

A sheriff's deputy stood guard outside another barrier of yellow tape designating the primary scene. He held a clipboard, and Jonah gave his name and rank for the record, which the man scribbled down. His expression was grim. "Ranger Foster, we don't know each other, but I've heard of you through the grapevine. Lots of people were talking after that school shooting last year. They say you're one of the best. This investigation might not get the same news attention as that one did, but I hope you'll take it just as seriously." An angry glint shimmered in the deputy's eyes. "Whoever did this needs to be punished."

The sheer rage pouring from the deputy caught Jonah off-guard. Kirkland County was small, and murder was heinous, but this level of emotion was out of the ordinary. First the suspicion of the deputy near the vehicles and now a lecture from... he checked the man's badge... Deputy Martinez.

"I can assure you, Deputy Martinez, I take all my cases seriously, no matter the victim or the level of media coverage. I'll do everything in my power to catch the perpetrator responsible."

He meant every word. Growing up as the overlooked middle child in a family of overachievers—Olympic athletes, doctors, business moguls—Jonah had spent most of his life feeling like he didn't measure up. He'd been aimless through most of college until a criminal justice class changed everything. The professor had been a retired detective who didn't lecture about glory or head-lines. Instead, he talked about the family who finally got answers after years of wondering what happened to their daughter and the father who could sleep again knowing his son's killer was behind bars.

That's when Jonah understood: law enforcement wasn't about chasing money or accolades. It was about helping people in their darkest moments.

Laney had been the first to encourage that choice. She'd shared his passion for service. They'd taken different routes—she went military while he joined the state troopers after graduation—but their core principles were the same. She understood him. Encouraged him. In a way that his family never had. Jonah knew his parents loved him, but to this day, they still couldn't understand why he'd spend 60 hours a week working for what amounted to a pitiful salary.

The attack on Laney made this case personal. But even if it hadn't been, Jonah would give it his all.

The deputy held his gaze for a moment, as if sizing him up, and then nodded. "We'll assist in any way we can."

"Thank you, Deputy."

Jonah ducked under the crime scene tape and joined Laney at the edge of the clearing. The faintest whiff of sun-dried cotton and something clean—like unscented soap and summer air—teased his nose. Laney was careful to avoid fragrant perfumes or body washes, anything that would attract bugs. The result was a freshness that was entirely her.

Unable to resist the urge to touch her, to confirm that she was there, whole and safe, he reached up and detangled the pine needle from her hair. Her dark strands were silky soft against his fingertips. Just a brief touch, but it caused his heart to skip a beat. The reaction was so familiar, Jonah often purposefully tuned it out. This time, he couldn't. Maybe it was more noticeable because an hour ago Denise had touched him and he'd felt nothing. Or maybe it was learning about the close call Laney suffered. Either way, the attraction caused a pang of longing in his chest.

He and Laney had dated briefly in college, but they'd been better as friends than a couple. Fifteen years later, he was grateful for that friendship, even if moments like this reminded him that his feelings had never been quite as platonic as he pretended.

Laney glanced at him, and her lips curved into a soft

smile before she ran her own fingers through her hair. "Thanks."

Jonah let the pine needle drift to the ground. "Mind telling me why the sheriff's deputies are on edge?"

Her smile faded as her features hardened. "One of the victims is the sheriff's niece."

That news was another gut-punch. Just when he thought this case couldn't get worse, it did.

"Sheriff Morrison has recused himself from the investigation," Laney continued. "He only has a handful of deputies, none of whom have the investigative experience to work this kind of case. That's why I called you." She squared her shoulders. "Ready to walk through it?"

He nodded, bracing himself for what was to come.

"When I arrived at the campsite, it was empty. No one answered when I called out. There was a fire in the pit and s'mores ingredients out, so I knew they hadn't gone far. A brief search led me to the first victim." She led Jonah across the clearing to the other side of a large tent. A young male lay on the ground, blood staining his shirt. A coroner's technician was taking photographs. "Tyler Chen, 21 years old and a student at the local university. Majoring in computer science. Shot twice in the back."

So young. Jonah smothered the anger welling inside him and focused on the area around the body. The dirt and pine needles were disturbed. Bloodstains spattered the side of the tent. He'd seen enough crime scenes to make a logical guess. "He was running when he was shot."

Laney nodded. "I surmised the same." She ruffled Scout's ears in a reassuring gesture when the canine whimpered. Naturally empathetic, the dog didn't like being around the deceased. It was a common reaction among search-and-rescue dogs. They took pride in finding people alive and could suffer from depression when that didn't happen. Even though Scout hadn't been "working" when Tyler died, she could still pick up on Laney's stress and sadness.

Broken branches and disturbed pine needles indicated a struggle. Jonah pointed to the area. "What happened there?"

"That's where I was attacked. The man wore a dark mask and clothing. He was athletic and fast, but I can't tell you his approximate height or weight." Frustration drew a furrow on her brow. "I can't even tell you his race."

"Eye color?"

She shook her head. "The eye holes of his balaclava were covered with dark mesh, and I couldn't see through it. Everything happened so fast. One minute I was looking at Tyler, and the next I was on the ground." Laney pointed to a bush. "My gun flew over there. I struck him with my flashlight, but he punched me, and the blow was enough to give him the advantage."

She swallowed hard as if fighting back memories. Once again, the urge to hug her rose, nearly overwhelming, but he knew now wasn't the time. Instead, he gave her a moment to gather herself. "What happened after Scout chased him away?"

"He took off toward the east, away from the lake. It wasn't until after he fled that I found the second victim." Laney followed a broken trail through the trees down to the water's edge. A young woman lay partially hidden in the high weeds. The beginning of a black eye marred her skin, and deep fingerprints bruised her neck. "Ava Morrison, the sheriff's niece. Also 21 and a college student."

Jonah drew in a deep breath and let it out slowly, forcing his mind to focus on the details of the crime scene. He noted the broken branches on nearby bushes, the footprints in the muck close to the shore, and Ava's ripped clothing. "You said a caller reported hearing fireworks at 9:15. Where is she located?"

"Campsite 5. She was driving past Campsite 8 when she heard the loud pops." Laney seemed to anticipate his question before he asked it. "No one is staying in Campsites 6, 7, or 9. Tyler and Ava were secluded out here."

Jonah suspected the killer had known that. He followed the trail back to the campsite. Laney and Scout joined him. Needing comfort, Jonah bent down and stroked the dog's head, smoothing her ears back before planting a kiss between her soulful brown eyes. She licked his hand.

Then he turned to face the campsite. Laney let him stew for a few moments and then asked, "What are you thinking?"

"The perpetrator snuck up on them. Came out of the woods holding a gun while they were making s'mores. Tyler and Ava ran. The killer shoots Tyler in the back, which explains the loud pops the caller mistook for fireworks as she was driving by. Then the perpetrator follows Ava into the woods, catching up with her at the lake. He sexually assaults her and then strangles her. Right about then is when you showed up. He hears you calling out to the campers." Jonah pointed to another path leading from the campsite. "Where does that go?"

"Campsite 9."

A theory formed in his mind. "Has anyone searched it?"

She shook her head. "Not to my knowledge."

"We need to. I bet we'll find evidence proving the killer parked there and used that path to enter this campsite. After killing Ava, he needed to get back to his vehicle, but you were in the way." He turned to face Laney. "That's why he attacked you."

She studied the scene. "Okay, that makes sense. But why strangle me if he had a gun?"

Jonah shrugged. "He strangled Ava. Maybe it's his preferred method when killing females. Or maybe he lost his gun in the weeds while attacking Ava. We'll do a thorough search of the area, see if we can find it." He sighed. "Where is the sheriff? I need to interview him."

"I convinced him to wait with a few deputies at the road." Laney stepped in front of him, her protective streak showing. "He's in rough shape, Jonah. Sheriff Morrison doesn't have kids of his own. His niece is his brother's only child. From what I've gathered, the entire family doted on her."

"I'll be sensitive, but the interview has to be done." He placed a hand on Laney's arm, stepping to the side and bringing her with him, so the coroner technicians could pass. They carried Tyler, wrapped in a black body bag, on a stretcher. "We need to interview both families to be sure, but my gut says Tyler was collateral damage." Determination fueled his words. "Ava was the real target. We need to find out why."

FOUR

Her throat ached and her head pounded in time with her heartbeat, but Laney's physical discomfort was slight compared to the pitch of her emotions at the sight of Sheriff Grayson Morrison. The proud lawman sat on the rear bumper of an SUV, shoulders hunched, eyes red-rimmed and bloodshot. He appeared devastated.

Chief Deputy Keisha Williams was speaking softly to him but looked up as they approached. Despite turning fifty last month, her sepia-colored skin remained unlined, and her figure athletic. Naturally curly hair was ruthlessly pulled back into a bun that fit her no-nonsense personality. She took several long strides in their direction, interrupting their progress.

"Laney." Williams nodded, then shifted her attention to Jonah. "You must be Texas Ranger Jonah Foster. Thank you for coming so quickly. I'm grateful for the assistance. Our department is dedicated to finding the perpetrator or perpetrators responsible. Whatever you need, just ask."

Jonah shook her hand. "Appreciate that, ma'am." He kept his voice pitched low. "If I may be frank, your deputies have been professional, but there's an underlying anger that's affecting their judgment. Deputy Martinez felt the need to lecture me about taking this case seriously, and another physically restrained me despite proper credentials. I understand why—this case hits close to home—but I need to know emotions won't compromise the investigation."

Williams looked toward the crime scene tape where her deputies stood rigid with barely controlled fury. "Point taken, Ranger Foster. I'll handle it."

A pang of irritation flared within Laney. The warning Jonah gave was unnecessary and hypocritical. This case was personal to him too, and no one was lecturing him about emotional distance. It was just like him to assume the worst. Yes, the deputies were upset, but these were good men who'd served their community faithfully for years. Martinez fished with the sheriff twice a month and had a teenage daughter of his own. Of course Ava's murder hit him hard. But that didn't make him a liability. It made him human.

"I assume you'll want to form a task force," Chief Deputy Williams continued. "My department will provide local support and manpower, but I think it makes sense for the Texas Rangers to lead the investigation itself."

Jonah gave a sharp nod. "There are a few issues that

need to be handled. It's possible the killer attacked Ranger Torres because he needed to cross through Campsite 8 in order to return to his vehicle. Please have a few of your deputies look around Campsite 9 for any potential evidence that needs to be preserved. I also want a thorough search around Ava's body to be conducted, as well as the trail leading back to Campsite 8. Specifically, I'm looking for—"

"The gun that killed Tyler. I've already thought of that, and it's being done. I'll have a couple of deputies check Campsite 9 as well."

"Good. I'd also like to interview Sheriff Morrison." He cast a glance toward Grayson, who sat with his head in his hands. "Would it be better to do it down at the station?"

The chief deputy's mouth flattened. "He refuses to leave until Ava's body has been removed from the scene." She sighed. "I doubt you'll be able to get anything useful out of him. He doesn't seem to know why anyone would want to kill Ava or Tyler."

Laney's heart broke for the sheriff. Their paths crossed on occasion professionally, and she'd always found him to be a solid lawman, but it was Grayson's dedication to his family that stuck with her the most. He'd been married to his wife for nearly fifty years, and whenever he'd spoken of his niece Ava, it'd been with immense pride.

Chief Deputy Williams led the way to the SUV and made introductions. Maybe it was Laney's imagination, but she wasn't sure the sheriff registered anything around him. Grief had already etched new lines on his forehead.

Laney laid a hand on his shoulder. "I'm so sorry for your loss, sheriff, and I know this is a difficult time, but we need to ask you some questions."

His blurry gaze snagged on the bruises on her neck before shifting to Jonah. For the first time, he seemed to register the Texas Ranger's presence. He blinked and straightened his shoulders, anger sparking. "I already know what you're going to ask, so let me say it succinctly. I don't know why anyone would want to murder Tyler or my niece. Neither of them were into drugs or anything illegal. They're good kids." His voice choked up. "Whoever did this targeted them randomly."

"Right now, nothing is off the table, but, sir, you and I both know the chances of this being a random crime are slim." Jonah's tone was gentle, but firm. "How long have Ava and Tyler been dating?"

"Since freshman year of college."

"Any problems in the relationship? Any recent breakups?"

"None. They were solid. Neither of them have an ex that would do something like this, and their friend group is pretty small. Tyler had an end-of-the-school-year party a few months back at my house. Invited his family, Ava's family, and a bunch of their friends. No one stuck out as odd or gave me a weird vibe." He scrubbed a hand over his face. "I know you need to ask these questions, Ranger Foster, but I'm not a civilian. I'd tell you if I knew anything that would be helpful."

"I have no doubt about that, sir." Jonah pressed on. "Neither Ava nor Tyler mentioned getting into a fight with someone? Or having a hard time with a friend?"

"No. Obviously I would say if they had."

"Do you know the password to Ava's cell phone?"

The sudden shift in questioning seemed to throw the sheriff off for a moment. He blinked. "Uhhh, no, but I'm sure her mother does." His expression crumpled. "My sister... Ava's parents are in town to visit her. They're staying at my house." His attention shot to his chief deputy, and he rose slightly. "Keisha, I want to be there—"

"We'll tell them together." The chief deputy waved him back down before turning toward Jonah and Laney. "Tyler's dad is deceased, but his mom lives in Fort Worth. I'll have the local PD notify her of his death and plan for her to be interviewed over the phone, or if she comes to town, in person."

Death notifications were one of the worst parts of being in law enforcement. Laney had only done a few, and each one had ripped out a piece of her heart. She still prayed for those families. Ava and Tyler's would be added to that list. This case was already one she'd never forget, and it had little to do with the fact that her life had been threatened.

Movement out of the corner of Laney's eye caught her attention. She turned in time to see her sister, Breanna, approach the yellow crime tape at a frenetic pace. Following on her heels was Marcus, Breanna's husband, dressed in basketball shorts and a T-shirt.

Strapped to his chest was a baby sling. A tuft of black hair was all that was visible of little Asher.

Laney excused herself and moved to intercept them, Scout at her side. "What are you guys doing here?" She ducked under the tape and was immediately embraced by her sister.

"We came to check on you." Breanna squeezed her tight and then backed up, her dark-eyed gaze sweeping over Laney's neck. She winced. "Papa Earl got a call from another ranger who said you'd been attacked. Are you okay?"

Papa Earl was Breanna's father-in-law. He'd worked as a park ranger at Piney Woods, and although he'd retired nearly two decades ago, he still had connections to the park. Namely, Andy Dawson. Her second-in-command probably called to reassure her family before they heard about it on the news. Something Laney should have thought of.

"I'm fine," she reassured her sister. "Just some bruises. Y'all shouldn't have driven all the way here. A phone call would've been sufficient."

Marcus held up his hands in mock surrender. "Don't look at me. I tried to tell Breanna that, but when your sister decides to do something, there's no talking her out of it. You're lucky I convinced her to let me drive."

"I was too upset to get behind the wheel of a car. As for you—" Breanna hugged Laney again tightly. Her voice thickened with tears. "I had to come and make sure you were okay. Calling wouldn't be enough. Your leg could be chopped off, and you'd say it was nothing but a flesh wound."

Laney chuckled, but her chest squeezed tight as her own emotions rose up to choke her. Breanna was all the family she had left. Their father had walked out when they were kids, choosing his mistress over his daughters. Their mom had passed away two years ago after battling cancer. Laney had always been close with her younger sister, even with a six-year age difference, but the losses had deepened their connection.

"Well, now that you know that I'm whole and mostly unharmed, you can take your husband and Asher back home." Laney kissed her sister's cheek.

Both Breanna and Marcus sported dark circles under their eyes. They'd had a lot of sleepless nights since Asher was born four months ago. Along with the new baby, Marcus's dad had moved in with the couple this summer. Papa Earl suffered from Parkinson's and recently had a stroke. Breanna was working herself to the bone taking care of him and the baby. Marcus was a great husband and father, but he was also the sole provider for their household at the moment. He picked up a lot of extra shifts at the hospital where he worked as a nurse.

Breanna wiped a tear from her cheek and squinted. "Is that Jonah with Sheriff Morrison?"

"Yes, he's helping with the investigation." It was a half-truth, since Jonah was actually leading the investigation, but Laney couldn't share details yet. Not before the families had been notified. She gave a half-hug to Marcus and kissed sleeping Asher on his sweet head. "Go home, guys. Get some rest. We'll talk more tomorrow."

She walked with them to their car and waved as they left. When she turned, Jonah was heading in her direction. Six four, and a lean two hundred pounds, he cut an imposing figure. Shadows darkened his blond hair into a lighter shade of gray and played across his carved cheekbones. Soft was never a word used to describe him. Except Laney knew the truth. Underneath that hard exterior, those scowls and grumpy attitude, was a sensitive soul. He journaled almost daily. Always remembered her birthday and never failed to think of a thoughtful gift. Would stay up late to game with her online.

And all of that tenderness was on full display when he came to a stop in front of her. His blue eyes scanned her face before flickering toward the retreating taillights of Marcus's truck. "Was that Breanna? Everything okay?"

"Yes. She just came to check on me. Did Sheriff Morrison have anything helpful to say?"

"No. Chief Deputy Williams requested she be the one to interview Ava's parents, since they know each other. I figured there was no harm in it. We all want to find the person responsible for this. Still, it's going to be a long night. I don't want to leave the scene until forensics is finished."

"There's a free cabin next to mine." Laney lived on site, in a small two-bedroom on the lake. Housing was a perk offered to park rangers at Piney Woods, but many didn't accept. The cabins were rustic, and living on the grounds meant being the first called when there was an issue. Laney had never minded. She loved her job, and now, as acting superintendent, it was a lot easier to handle urgent matters if she was on site at all times. "You can crash there while the investigation is ongoing."

Jonah kept a go-bag in his truck at all times, and like her, he lived simply. His apartment was bare-bones, so the accommodations wouldn't bother him. He flashed her a slight smile. "Thanks."

They were standing near Jonah's truck. Laney leaned against it. She was more tired, and more emotionally drained, than she wanted to admit. Seeing Breanna's distress and panic had driven home just how close she'd come to losing her life tonight. It was taking everything to hold herself together.

As if Scout could sense her distress, she pressed her body against Laney's leg before sitting on her foot. The dog's solid presence was reassuring, but Jonah's nearness threatened to expose her raw emotions. She bit her lip to keep from crying, thankful for the deep shadows and the other vehicles. They hid her crumbling composure from the other law enforcement.

Jonah hesitated. "Laney... I know you don't want to talk about it now, but when you do, I'm here."

She swallowed down the lump in her throat. "I already know that."

"Yeah, but it helps to hear it out loud. So does this." Jonah tugged her into his strong arms. He smelled of laundry soap and peppermints. His embrace was familiar and grounding. He breathed out, long and low, as if the mere act of holding her was a reassurance.

She held on, still fighting back her tears. "Don't make me cry, Jonah, or I'll never forgive you."

"A good cry is what you need sometimes."

"Oh yeah? When's the last time you had one?"

"Pretty sure it was when you broke up with me."

She heard the buried smile in his voice. "Liar." She pulled in a deep breath and let the solidness of her best friend's presence soothe her. "You and I made a terrible couple."

They saw the world in different ways. Jonah was a pessimist where she was an optimist, he was fond of reading and quiet nights in, while she enjoyed socializing and parties. Their relationship had only lasted a month, but interspersed with their silly fights and different worldviews were deep conversations and genuine respect. Laney had never been one to drag her feet when breaking things off, but with Jonah, it'd been difficult. And when he asked if they could still be friends, she was relieved, but hesitant. She hadn't known if he truly meant it.

But he had.

Over the next fifteen years, Jonah had become a fixture in her life. They'd supported each other through everything. Career changes, the end of relationships, losing loved ones. He was her date to weddings. Late-night conversations, trips all over the US, care packages when she was on deployment, and the occasional fight had cemented their relationship. Years ago, early in his career, Jonah had been shot and injured in the line of duty. Laney dropped everything to move in and take care of him. She knew he'd do the same for her in a heartbeat. Other than Breanna, Jonah was the only person in the world she relied on. He'd never let her down.

Which was exactly why she'd called him to head up this case.

She sighed. "I'm glad you're here."

"Me too." He brushed a kiss on the top of her head and then released her. His gaze dropped to the bruises on her neck, and he grimaced. "Your injuries need to be photographed for the record, and you need to give an official statement of what happened."

He was right. She knew that. But Laney couldn't be in a room with someone—even another professional—and bare herself in that way. It was too... vulnerable. She licked her lips. "Will you do it?"

"Of course."

His voice was soft, but the shadows hid his expression. A strange tension filled the air. Laney's heart skipped a beat. She sensed there were things Jonah wasn't saying, things hovering just beneath the surface of his careful control. And for a moment, she was tempted to step back into his embrace. To hold on and not let go.

But she didn't. Laney couldn't afford to.

She'd learned long ago that romance didn't last. Promises could be broken. Forever wasn't guaranteed. Just as vividly as Laney could remember building her first fire with her dad, she could recall the day he walked out the door, suitcase in hand. Overnight, he became a stranger who chose his mistress over his wife and daughters.

Her mother had never been the same after their dad left. She'd cried for weeks and struggled to get out of bed. When she finally pulled herself together, it'd only been for the sake of her two girls. She'd done everything possible to be a good mother, but there was a hollowness to Eileen Torres that never went away. Laney could still remember sitting on the stairs during a visit home one Christmas, nearly two decades after her father left, and watching her mother stifle sobs late at night while looking at her wedding album.

Some betrayals cut too deep to be mended. Some risks were too great to take.

So she kept the line drawn. Friendship was safe. Anything more was a gamble she couldn't take.

Even with Jonah.

Especially with Jonah.

FIVE

Jonah groaned as a wet nose touched his cheek. He opened one eye to find Scout staring intently. She took advantage of his prone state to swipe a kiss over his mouth and cheek. He gently pushed the dog away. "Gross. Scout, we're friends, but we're not that close." Squeezing his eyes shut against the daylight streaming through his window, he buried himself under the blankets. "Go back to Laney."

His cell phone blared from the nightstand. *Happy* by Pharrell Williams. Laney's special ringtone, which she'd programmed into his phone. The tune was irritatingly positive, and he kept meaning to change it, but never remembered to.

He grabbed the cell phone. Hitting answer without cracking open an eye, he growled. "What?"

"Good morning to you too, Sunshine. Time to wake up. We've got lots to do."

He squinted at the time on his phone and groaned.

Seven in the morning. He'd planned to be up at six but must've slept through his alarm. Three hours of sleep was all he'd had, most of it spent at the hospital while they photographed Laney's injuries and a doctor examined her throat. It was going to be a rough day. Jonah rolled over on the lumpy mattress. "I'm up."

"Liar."

Scout jumped on the bed and licked his face again. "Scout!" He held up an arm to ward her off before sitting up. "I'm awake, okay. Call off your dog." He glowered at Scout, who wagged her tail. "How did you get into the cabin anyway?"

"I have an extra key." Laughter filled Laney's voice. "Hurry up. Your coffee is getting cold."

She hung up. He grumbled as he untwisted the blankets from his legs. Scout hopped off the mattress and pranced toward the doorway. He shook his head. "Hold on, pup. Gotta take care of business first." He used the bathroom. His hair stuck up in spikes, and his cheek still held a crease mark from the pillow. He studied his reflection blearily while brushing his teeth. Good grief, was that a touch of gray in his stubble? On days like these, he felt far older than thirty-six.

Barefoot, he exited the bathroom and followed Scout through the small living room to a tiny kitchen. She waited patiently for him to open the back door and then bounded off the porch into the backyard where Laney waited. She was dressed for the day in a fresh uniform, the silky strands of her hair pulled back into a neat pony-tail. A touch of lip gloss was her only makeup. The bruises on her neck were darker now—deep purple fingerprints that made his jaw tighten. Jonah stuffed his feet into his boots and stepped outside.

"Your coffee." She pointed to a mug perched on the railing. "I made it thick enough to be soup and strong enough to grow hair between your toes, just the way you like it."

Jonah ignored her teasing. He took a long drink from the mug, letting the dark brew spark his brain awake. The grass was damp with dew, the air moist against his bare arms. Light cloud cover hid the brightest rays of the sun, which kept the temperature pleasant, but humidity was already building, promising another sweltering Texas day. Below the slope of the yard was the lake. Dragonflies flitted on the surface.

He breathed in the pine-scented air before taking another sip of coffee. Laney picked up a ball and tossed it. Scout took off running. Her tail bounced as she dove into some bushes.

For a moment, it almost felt normal. Like any other morning they'd spent together over the years.

Then Laney's expression shifted, and the illusion shattered.

"I have something to show you, and you're not going to like it." She glanced at him. "I debated leaving it until after breakfast, but you'd be angrier if I waited."

His muscles tensed. "What is it?"

"Early this morning, around four, Scout was agitated. She kept pacing in front of the back door. She's never done that before, so I knew something was wrong.

Initially, I thought it was an animal. Maybe a deer coming up close to the cabin." She led him down a small path through the woods to the lake, coming to a stop next to a willow tree. The moss hanging from the branches swayed in the light breeze. "But then on my morning walk, I found this."

She pointed to the tamped-down grass and clear drag marks leading from the water's edge. "Someone brought a small canoe or kayak onto shore here. Could be from last night, could be more recent. But given Scout's behavior and the timing..."

"Someone approached your house." The words came out flat, but fury coiled beneath them. Jonah scanned the shoreline, then the open water. A few small boats and scattered kayaks dotted the glassy surface—fishermen out for a morning catch, pontoon boats prepping for family outings, rowers squeezing in exercise before the heat became unbearable.

The lake was man made, a reservoir fed by the Colorado River, and crossed several jurisdictions. Part of it belonged to Piney Woods State Park, but other sections were privately owned or accessible through county-managed parks.

He turned back to Laney. "You should have called me the second Scout alerted. At four in the morning."

"First of all, I wasn't certain there was trouble. Second, you were dead on your feet and needed the sleep. And third, I'm a law enforcement officer too." Her chin lifted. "Former military, I might add. I can handle myself."

"I know what you are." The words came out sharper than he'd intended. Jonah pulled in a breath and tempered his tone. "But after what happened last night, you should have called. I was fifty feet away, Laney."

She chewed on the inside of her cheek and then blew out a breath. "Okay. Maybe I should have called out of an abundance of caution." Her gaze narrowed. "But you're also being overprotective."

"You got that right. And I make no apologies for it."

She threw up her hands in exasperation. "You're the most infuriating person to argue with. Can we focus on what's important? If this was the killer, he knows the area well enough to have brought his boat up to shore and found the trail that leads to my cabin. He's a local. Probably a frequent camper or outdoorsman. Someone who spends a great deal of time in the park."

An icy finger of dread touched the back of his neck. "Someone you might know."

She met his gaze. "Yes. Maybe he's worried I'll remember something about the attack, some detail that can identify him. Which is good. That means he's scared and may make a mistake."

It could also make her a target. "Laney, you need to be careful—"

"Okay, we've reached the lecture part of the morning." She hooked an arm through his, the gesture so familiar it sent an ache through his chest. "I have breakfast burritos. You're impossible to deal with when you're hungry."

And she thought he was infuriating to argue with?

Jonah allowed her to tug him back down the path toward her cabin. Scout bounced ahead, tail wagging. "I'm not some troll under a bridge you have to throw food and coffee at."

"Umm... okay."

The smile playing on her lips was irresistible. Jonah's irritation at her unwillingness to discuss her safety faded, but not his worry. Laney kept up a steady stream of chatter as they followed the path back to her cabin. Nothing terribly important. A bird song she recognized, the desire for rain, a funny story about her sister and Asher. The sound of her lilting voice soothed the rough edges of his emotions.

The kitchen smelled of bacon. Jonah crossed to the coffeepot on the counter in three strides and poured more of the dark brew into his empty mug. Laney hummed as she pulled an egg carton and other ingredients from the fridge. Her cabin, like his, was rustic, but she'd added personality. Her dishtowel was teal and matched the mug in his hand. Photographs of her family were attached to the fridge with magnets. His own smiling image reflected back from several of the pictures, a testament to the long history of their friendship. He scanned the cluster of photos almost without thinking, but there were no recent additions.

Jonah stole a slice of pepper from the cutting board and popped it in his mouth. Masochist that he was, he asked, "How's Mike?"

Mike O'Neill had been Laney's longest boyfriend. Six months and going. Jonah had a hard time understanding why he'd stuck when Laney had been quick to get rid of everyone else—himself included—but there it was.

Laney flipped on the burner. "Mike and I broke up last month."

A secret jolt of pleasure shot through him, followed immediately by a familiar warning. *Don't go there.* Laney cycled through boyfriends like most people changed seasons—always friendly breakups, always "just not quite right." He'd watched her do it for fifteen years and had already been a casualty in her pattern of keeping things light and breezy. Their friendship depended on steering clear of romance.

The corner of his mouth lifted in a half-grin. "Did you tire of discussing programming hacks and Star Trek movies?"

"Don't be mean. Mike was sweet, but we didn't have much in common. Honestly, the relationship only lasted as long as it did because we didn't see each other much. I've been so busy, especially since Superintendent Voss went on medical leave, that dating has been a vague memory." She poured the egg mixture into the frying pan. "The summer rush is finally over, and I'd hoped things would settle down, but it doesn't look like that's going to be the case now. Have you heard from Chief Deputy Williams?"

"Yes." He'd read the string of text messages from the chief deputy before heading out to the yard. "No one in the family has any idea why someone would want to kill Ava. No troublesome exes. Neither she nor Tyler were into drugs or anything illegal. As Sheriff Morrison asserted, they were good kids. But we have to take what the family says with a grain of salt. They may not have known what was going on with Ava or Tyler."

"It didn't look like a drug hit to me. I agree with your assessment that Ava was the target. The killer took his time with her. Sexually assaulted her, and then instead of shooting her as he had Tyler, he strangled her. That's up close and personal."

He nodded. It bothered him. The intimacy of the murder. If Ava had an ex, he'd be the first one questioned, but she'd been dating Tyler for years. Had she attracted a stalker and not known it? It was something to think about.

Jonah opened a cabinet and removed plates. "Deputies found the gun, by the way. A Ruger SR9 with a suppressor."

"A suppressor? That explains why the camper who called it in reported fireworks."

He nodded. A suppressor didn't make the gunshots silent, they just reduced the noise significantly.

"Where did the deputies find the weapon?" Laney asked.

"It'd fallen into the lake near Ava's body. The water likely destroyed any fingerprints or DNA, but the lab will take a pass at it anyway. And there were clear signs someone had parked a vehicle in Campsite 9. The undergrowth was crushed. Deputies also found fresh tire rubber on a tree where someone had scraped against it backing in, and there was an oil spot on the packed earth."

"So you were right. The killer attacked me in order to get back to his vehicle." She frowned. "What bothers me is the timing. How did the killer know Tyler and Ava would be at that remote campsite? It's not that Campsite 8 is popular or well-known. Someone either followed them there or knew their plans."

Laney handed him a plate loaded down with a breakfast burrito and fruit. "I think we should prioritize interviewing Ava's friends. It could help us narrow down which people knew her and are also familiar enough with the park to pull off a murder like this. If the killer is coming after me because he's afraid that I'll recognize him, then we're looking for someone both Ava and I know."

The thought that someone in her daily circle might be a killer made his blood run cold. Laney was smart and tough, but she also believed in the goodness of people. An optimist through and through. How was he supposed to protect her from someone she trusted? Someone she might let her guard down with?

Her cell phone beeped. She checked the screen and grimaced. "I have a meeting today with Superintendent Voss. I completely forgot."

Her boss. He was currently on medical leave while receiving cancer treatment. "Can you cancel it?"

"I could, but I need to go into headquarters to address the park rangers before they start their shifts. The local news channel has already picked up the story."

She gestured to the television in the living room. It was playing silently, tuned to a morning news show. A reporter was broadcasting from the lake with the caption: Double Murder at Piney Woods. The image changed to photographs of Tyler and Ava, embracing and laughing. Happy.

Jonah's chest tightened. Two young people with their whole lives ahead of them, reduced to a news caption and crime scene photos. He couldn't bring them back. All he could do now was make sure their killer faced justice.

"Campers will be flooding the visitor's center with calls and visits. I've already sent out an email to the staff, informing them about the deaths and instructing them not to speak to the media, but they'll have questions and concerns that need to be addressed." She rubbed her forehead as if a headache was coming on. "Will you want to do interviews?"

"Yes, starting with whoever checked them in when they arrived." Jonah steered Laney to the table and gently pushed her into a chair. "But first, breakfast. Otherwise, I won't be the only cranky one."

Her lips quirked. "Heaven forbid."

They joined hands, bent their heads, and blessed the food. They'd done this hundreds of times over the years, but for some inexplicable reason, this time, Jonah was achingly aware of the softness of Laney's skin. Silently, he offered an extra prayer.

God, please help me keep her safe.

SIX

Forty minutes later, fortified by the breakfast burrito and another cup of coffee, Laney pushed through the main doors of the visitor center. The rustic wood-and-stone building blended into the natural background. It smelled of cedar and fresh coffee. Sunlight streamed through the wide front windows, pooling across polished concrete floors and catching on the glass display case of local wildlife exhibits. In the corner, a stuffed great horned owl kept silent watch over a rack of trail maps, its glass eyes as sharp as the real thing.

"Morning, boss." Brett Harrison greeted her from behind the reception desk. At six-foot-two with an easy smile and sun-weathered features, Brett had an approachable, All-American look that made visitors feel instantly at ease. His sandy hair was perpetually wind-blown, and his athletic build suggested someone who spent more time hiking trails than sitting behind a desk. At twenty-eight, he was one of the younger staff members, but he carried himself with quiet confidence. Most people found him instantly likeable.

Scout, however, kept her distance. Her tail stilled, and she positioned herself slightly behind Laney's legs. It was a reaction she sometimes had to certain men, though Laney had never quite figured out the pattern.

His gaze dropped to her neck and the bruises there. He winced. "Oof. Those look painful."

"They look worse than they feel."

She greeted the group of on-duty rangers and various staff that'd gathered in the lobby before their shift, as she'd requested. Around thirty people. Labor Day weekend was always one of their busiest times, and she'd scheduled extra staff to handle the traffic. Laney introduced Jonah and then got down to business. On Saturdays, the visitor center opened at nine. Campers and visitors would learn about the murders—if they hadn't already—and would need reassurance.

"Due to last night's events, our visitors will be understandably alarmed and concerned. Chief Deputy Williams will hold a press conference later today, but as of right now, the investigation is ongoing. What we can say is this: the incident appears to be isolated, and there is no reason to believe the public is in danger. However, we will be taking additional safety precautions. The Texas Rangers are working in coordination with our office and the Kirkland County Sheriff's Department. As more information becomes available and I'm able to, I will share it. Please do not engage with the media and do not answer a reporter's questions about the murders. Be polite but answer with a simple no comment. Questions?"

There were a few moments of shifting as the group looked at each other. Then tentatively, Ranger Zoe Papadopoulos raised her hand. "Is it possible the killer is staying here in the park?"

Laney hesitated. She didn't want to alarm her staff, but they needed to use caution. "It is possible. Use caution when interacting with visitors, and for the time being, we will patrol in teams of two."

She fielded several more questions, and then paused, taking a moment to meet everyone's eyes. She wasn't used to being the boss. Laney had been a park ranger for years, and after coming to Piney Woods, worked alongside Andy as Deputy Ranger. But she'd always had someone above her to call the shots. Leadership wasn't something she took lightly, and the weight of responsibility felt heavy on her shoulders, especially now.

"I know this is frightening. Two young people lost their lives in our park, and that shakes all of us. But we do our jobs because we believe in protecting this place and the people who visit it. That hasn't changed. We're going to stay vigilant, stay together, and we're going to help law enforcement catch whoever did this."

The tension in the room eased slightly. Zoe nodded, her shoulders squaring. A few of the rangers exchanged glances, determination replacing the worry in their expressions.

She gestured toward Chief Ranger Andy Dawson. His shock of white hair was neatly combed, but the bags under his eyes gave him a hangdog appearance. "Chief Ranger Dawson will give you your new assignments."

The briefing broke up, and the lobby began to empty. That's when she noticed her boss, Douglass Voss, sitting in a chair on the other side of the room. Scout, tail wagging, approached him. She promptly sat and was rewarded with a shower of affection. Scout had always loved Douglass.

Laney turned to Jonah. "I need a few minutes to meet with Douglass and Andy. There's a small conference room over there. You're welcome to use it for the time being."

He nodded. "I have some phone calls to make." With a gentle squeeze of her arm, he headed for the conference room. She watched his confident strides for a beat too long before realizing Brett had been watching the interaction from his position behind the desk.

Jonah's light touch hadn't been out of place, but Laney's cheeks still heated, as if Brett had caught them doing something improper. She forced a smile despite her embarrassment and gave a sharp nod before crossing the lobby to greet Douglass. "Good morning, sir."

Douglass, using the arms of the chair for assistance, rose. He was thinner and frailer than she'd seen him last. The chemotherapy treatments had thinned his hair. But his smile was warm and fatherly, scrunching the crow's feet fanning his eyes. "Laney, it's good to see you, although I wish it were under better circumstances."

"So do I." She met Andy's eye and tilted her head to indicate he should join them before leading Douglass back to her office. She kept the conversation on lighter topics, asking about his wife and children, while they settled in the seating area next to floor-to-ceiling windows overlooking the lake. Once Andy had joined them, she shifted to more serious matters. "What can I do for you, sir?"

"I'm taking early retirement."

Laney blinked. A quick look at Andy revealed he didn't seem the least bit surprised. He'd known. She waited a beat and then carefully said, "I'm sorry, sir, I don't understand. When we spoke last week on the phone, you said treatment was going well. Has something changed?"

"No, no, the treatment is going very well." He smiled gently. "In fact, I'm due to finish my last chemo tomorrow. But my wife and I have had a lot of time to think and talk. We want to travel once I'm in remission. Enjoy more time with our grandkids. I have retirement from the military and enough years with the park service to receive my full pension. It seems silly to put our adventures on hold."

Laney could sympathize with his wish to spend more time with his family. When her mother was diagnosed with cancer, she'd packed up her life and moved home. Thankfully, there'd been a ranger position open at Piney Woods. Douglass had hired her on the spot. She would miss him. "The staff will be sorry to see you go, sir, myself included."

"Thank you." Douglass studied her with the scrutiny of a seasoned law enforcement officer. Like her, he'd spent time as an MP before becoming a park ranger, and while chemo may have taken the edge off his strength, it hadn't diminished his sharp instincts. "My retirement, of course, means the superintendent position will be available. I want to recommend to the TDPW that your promotion be made permanent. It's not a guarantee that you'll be offered the position, but given your exceptional record, they'd be hard pressed to find someone better."

"Especially since I will second Douglass's recommendation," Andy added.

Shock rendered her speechless. Laney's gaze shifted between the two men. Clearly, this was something they'd discussed ahead of time. She felt ambushed. Competing emotions battled for her attention. Excitement and terror. She chose her words carefully. "I'm honored that you would recommend me. Both of you." She frowned. "But wouldn't you be the better choice, Andy? You have more years of experience."

"I'm closing in on retirement myself. I'll stay on as your Chief Ranger for the next two years to ensure the ship stays on course, but Piney Woods needs fresh energy. Leadership with vision and a passion to take on new projects." His mouth quirked. "And I don't want to spend my time buried in the extra paperwork."

She chuckled. Laney didn't like the paperwork any more than he did.

Silence settled in the room. Laney felt the walls closing in. Not literally, but the weight of permanence pressed against her chest. *Superintendent.* Not acting. Not temporary. *Permanent.* The word tasted like a trap.

She drew in a breath. "Again, I'm honored that you

both would recommend me. I'd like a bit of time to consider the matter." She smiled wryly. "There's a lot on my mind at the moment."

"Of course. I don't plan on turning in the paperwork for my retirement for another few weeks." Douglass rose and extended his hand.

Laney shook it warmly. "Thank you, sir. I mean that."

"No need to thank me, Laney. You stepped up when we needed you most. That tells me everything I need to know about the kind of leader you'll be."

With a final handshake and a pat on Scout's head, Douglass left the office, escorted by Andy. Their voices filtered down the hall as they moved to the lobby. Laney crossed the room to her desk and sank into her chair. She stared out of the window at the pine trees and the lake. A couple climbed into a canoe and pushed off from the boathouse.

Superintendent. Superintendent Torres. She wasn't sure what to think of it.

A knock on her doorframe drew her attention. Jonah strolled in, his long legs eating up the distance to her desk. "I spoke to Chief Deputy Williams. She's—" He paused, a slight crease forming between his brows. "What's wrong?"

"Nothing. I..." Laney debated not saying anything, but this was Jonah. Her best friend. She told him everything.

Well, almost everything.

"Douglass is taking an early retirement. He wants to

recommend to headquarters that they keep me on as superintendent."

A wide grin broke out across Jonah's face, transforming his normally serious features. It was the kind of smile that made people—especially women—do double-takes. Genuine and unguarded in a way he rarely allowed. It sent warmth straight through her.

"That's amazing, Laney! Congrats." He paused, seeming to register that she wasn't as thrilled with the news as he was. His smile dimmed. "Or not? This is great news, so why do you look like someone threw up on your shoes?"

"Because I'm not sure I'm going to accept the offer. I moved here because Mom was sick. After she passed, there was Breanna's wedding, and then she was pregnant with Asher and..."

"You just stayed," he filled in.

Laney tucked a strand of hair behind her ear. "She needed me. Still does. But I won't lie, there's an urge to move on. I couldn't do that if I was Superintendent. It's more responsibility."

"You don't think you'll ever settle down in one spot?"

There was something in the depths of his blue eyes that made her stomach flutter. Jonah's tone was casual, but the question seemed loaded for some strange reason.

She averted her gaze and shrugged, keeping her voice light. "I enjoy meeting new people. Facing different challenges." She'd moved dozens of times. Her career in the military had required it, but even as a park ranger, she'd hopped to a new assignment every few years. Already she was feeling antsy. Truth be told, Laney intended to move on to another park once Douglass came back to work.

"There's a benefit to staying in one place though," Jonah said. "You can create deeper friendships and be a more meaningful part of a community. Maybe meet someone, get married, and have a family of your own."

A few years ago, Laney would have laughed at the idea of settling down. Somehow, seeing her younger sister happily married with a baby... it'd unearthed a desire for a future she'd never considered before. It also ignited, in equal measure, a pit-in-her-stomach terror. "The longest relationship I've ever had lasted six months. Wedding bells aren't even on my radar." A thought stilled her movements. "Do you think about it? Getting married?"

"It's crossed my mind a time or two." His voice was low, loaded with some unspoken emotion she couldn't quite place. Jonah's mouth quirked. "Of course, I'd have to find someone who can put up with me."

Laney chuckled. "There's that. You're a handful, Foster." Her tone was light, but a sinking feeling settled in her belly at the thought of him getting married. She'd never considered it. Jonah didn't date much, and his serious relationships had been few and far between.

Still... how foolish of her. Deep down, Jonah had always been a romantic. He was considerate and kind. Smart. Good with kids. Definitely easy on the eyes. Any woman in her right mind would be lucky to marry him. Would his wife be comfortable with their friendship? Some women wouldn't be. Regardless, Jonah's first duty would be to his wife. Things would change between them, and selfishly, Laney didn't want them to.

This train of thought wasn't helping anyone. Shifting back to more comfortable ground, she said, "What were you about to tell me? About Chief Deputy Williams?"

"She's going to interview Ava and Tyler's family members again, as well as their friends. Since it's Labor Day weekend, a lot of the college kids have gone home or are on vacation, but she's tracking down everyone she can. I also spoke with my boss, Lieutenant Rodriguez. She's sending Ryker and Tate to assist us on the case. They'll be here tomorrow."

Texas Rangers Ryker Montgomery and Tate Atwood were both members of Company A. Laney had never worked with either man in a professional setting, but she knew them well socially. She'd watched Ryker and Hannah exchange marriage vows just two months ago, and even she—cynic that she was—had felt a flicker of hope watching them. But hope was dangerous. While she didn't believe for a second Ryker would ever leave Hannah for another woman, that didn't prevent something else from tearing them apart in a few years.

"I thought Ryker was in Hawaii on his honeymoon."

"Got back last night."

She winced. "Hannah can't be happy about us stealing him away. The man barely had time to unpack."

"Are you kidding me?" He eyed her incredulously. "Have you checked your cell phone recently?"

Laney pulled the device from her pocket. She'd put her cell on silent for the meeting with her staff and

Douglass, and was stunned to see 30 new text messages. Rangers from Company A—along with their wives and significant others—all texted their support, prayers, and offers to help. Hannah was among them. The demonstration of love was overwhelming. "That's... wow."

"They care about you."

"Clearly." She shot off a message to the group, thanking them, and then arched a brow. "I wonder... how many text messages did you receive?" The corners of her mouth lifted even though Laney battled against it. Teasing Jonah was one of her favorite pastimes, mainly because he made it so easy.

He scowled. "They like you better than they like me. I know that already. You don't need to rub it in."

"They do not, and you know it. Although it might help matters if you smiled more."

"What? Change my sparkling personality? No thanks." Jonah gestured to her computer. "Can you log in and tell me who checked Ava and Tyler in when they arrived yesterday afternoon? And the exact time they checked in, along with any activities they registered for?"

"Trying to figure out who they ran into at the park?"

He nodded, leaning on her desk. "The incident this morning changes things a bit. If the killer is afraid you'll recognize him, then chances are it's someone who works here. I'd like to trace Ava and Tyler's movements in the park from the time they arrived until the murders."

"Okay." She logged into the system and navigated to the check-in log. Her finger scrolled down the screen until she found the entry. "Brett was at the front desk when they arrived. He's there now, so we can interview him. Looks like Tyler registered his vehicle, per policy, and got a parking tag for it. They also rented a two-person kayak from the boathouse."

"Sheriff Morrison mentioned Ava loved kayaking."

"Eddie Sorenson was working in the boathouse." She checked the schedule and frowned. "He's supposed to be here this morning, but I didn't see him at the staff meeting. Maybe he arrived late."

Jonah straightened. "Or maybe he didn't show up at all." His expression darkened. "After someone was lurking around your cabin this morning, I don't like coincidences. Let's find Eddie."

SEVEN

The boathouse was locked up tight, with a sign hanging from a nail on the front: *Be Back in Fifteen Minutes.* Sunlight beat down on Jonah's shoulders as he tried the handle anyway. Locked. "Could he still be inside even though it's locked?"

"Yes." Laney gestured for him to step aside and used a key from the ring on her belt. Scout waited patiently at her side, ears pricked.

Jonah gently pushed past her as the door swung open. "Let me go first."

She looked annoyed but didn't fight him on it.

The boathouse was dim and cool, water lapping at the edges of the dock. Kayaks and canoes lined up neatly on metal racks. Life jackets of various sizes hung from hooks along the far wall. Everything appeared in order, but there was no sign of Eddie.

The door swung shut behind them with a soft thud.

"Hello? Eddie?" Laney called out, moving past him

toward the small office in the corner. Its door stood open, light spilling out. She leaned in, then gestured to the computer. "He's logged in. And his truck's in the parking lot. He's definitely here."

The main entrance creaked open. A man entered, looking pale and drawn, sweat beading on his forehead. Eddie, Jonah presumed. He wore the staff uniform, which consisted of a polo shirt and cargo pants. His boots were dusty. Gray threaded through his hair at the temples. Despite his hunched shoulders, it was clear Eddie was in shape, with the tan of someone who spent a lot of time outdoors.

Scout scooted closer to Laney, taking a protective posture.

Eddie startled when he spotted them. "Good morning, ma'am." His gaze flickered to Jonah. "You must be Ranger Foster." He let the door swing shut behind him and approached with his hand outstretched. Eddie cast a wary look toward Scout, suggesting the mistrust was mutual.

Jonah shook Eddie's hand. "Nice to meet you."

"Same." He withdrew his hand and used the heel to wipe a bead of sweat from his forehead. "It's a scorcher out there today. I keep waiting for the weather to cool off, but it seems we might have to wait a bit longer."

"Where were you?" Laney's tone was polite, but her gaze sharp. "I noticed you clocked in late, and the boathouse is supposed to remain open."

"I went to the mess hall for something to settle my stomach." He lifted the ginger ale. "Been fighting some kind of stomach bug all morning. That's why I was late. Thought about calling in sick, but we're so short-staffed right now, I didn't want to leave you guys hanging."

Laney's posture relaxed slightly. Eddie, however, remained jittery. His attention jumped between his boss and Jonah. "Is something wrong? Is this about the murders? The staff was talking about it at the mess hall. Horrible."

"Yes, it is. The couple that died, Ava Morrison and Tyler Chen, rented a kayak yesterday afternoon." Laney glanced at Jonah, indicating he should take the lead, while simultaneously reaching down to pet Scout. The dog's posture remained stiff. "We wanted to ask you some questions about that."

"Of course. How can I help?"

Jonah decided to start off easy, hoping to put Eddie at ease and get him talking. "What time did they rent the kayak for?"

"Let me check." He headed into the office and used the mouse to navigate to the schedule. "Four in the afternoon. But I vaguely remember they were running late. I saw their photos on the news this morning and remembered them. They were so happy together. Laughing and joking. They seemed great together."

"Was anyone else in here when they arrived?"

"Uhhh, a family with two kids." Eddie stared at the ceiling as if he was running back through the events. "Yeah, yeah. I remember the young lady..."

"Ava," Laney supplied.

"Yeah, Ava." He gave Laney a soft smile of thanks.

"She helped one kid put on his lifejacket. She was a natural. I wanted to ask her to volunteer for us sometime, but then another couple came in and I forgot. We're pretty busy in the afternoon when school gets out. Lots of families and teens."

"Did you sense any tension between Ava and Tyler?" Jonah asked. "Notice anyone paying attention to them in any way?"

"No." Eddie popped open the can of ginger ale. "Like I said, they seemed great together. We went through the instructions, but it was brief. They both informed me they were regular kayakers. From the way they maneuvered out of the boathouse and onto the lake, they were telling the truth about that."

"And what time did they bring the kayak back?"

Eddie took a sip of his drink and consulted the schedule. "They had a two-hour rental, so it must've been around six. Could've been a bit before or after. Like I said, that time of day is busy for us. We close up at seven, so lots of people are returning their kayaks and canoes. Plus, the high school rowing team practice goes from three to six. It's mayhem."

Something felt off, but Jonah couldn't put his finger on what it was. Eddie had relaxed while they talked, but he fidgeted a lot. Nervous energy. It was the best way to describe it. Shuffling papers, taking a drink, his leg jittering. Could be the man had an abundance of energy—some people couldn't sit still—or it could be a sign that he was worried. Jonah didn't know him well enough to tell.

"After they returned the kayak, did you see Ava and Tyler later that night? At the mess hall, perhaps?"

"No. My shift ended a little after seven, and I went straight home."

Jonah glanced at his left hand. No wedding ring. "Do you live alone?"

Eddie stilled. "Why are you asking?"

"Routine questions. Nothing to worry about. We're asking them of everyone."

"Oh." He paused. "Yeah, I live alone. Ate a frozen dinner and watched a football game." Eddie rolled his eyes. "Not very exciting, but..." He shrugged. "I don't get out much."

"What game did you watch?"

"Cowboys and Eagles. Caught the second half."

An easy thing to verify. "See any of your neighbors around? Did you talk to anyone?"

His gaze dropped to the desk, and he fiddled with the tab on his ginger ale. "Nope."

Liar. But that didn't make him a killer. Jonah made a mental note to do a thorough background check. If he had a criminal record, it would have been flagged by the TDPW when he was hired, but that'd been years ago. How often were the backgrounds redone? He'd ask Laney later.

"Thanks for your help." Jonah extended a hand for Eddie to shake. "Hope you feel better soon."

"Appreciate it." Eddie appeared relieved to have the interview over.

"Are you sure you can complete your shift today?" Laney asked. "I can have someone else cover for you."

"I'll let you know if things get worse, but I'm okay for now." Eddie gave her a nod. "Thanks, though."

"Sure thing."

They stepped out of the boathouse and into the sunshine. Jonah's hat shielded his face, but his eyes squinted at the drastic change in light. The lake looked cool and inviting. Some ducks swam by, creating ripples on the smooth surface.

Laney made sure the boathouse door stayed open before joining him on the trail leading back to the visitor center. "What do you think?"

"He's lying about where he was last night, and he was jittery. How often do you recheck criminal records?"

"Rangers are checked annually, but administrative employees—like Eddie—are checked every five years."

"How long has he worked here?"

"About ten years."

"He doesn't like Scout much."

"No, but no one's perfect." Laney laid a hand on his arm, pulling him to a stop under the shade of an oak tree. "Eddie's an outstanding employee. He gets top marks on his reviews every time. He's a team player, and to my knowledge, no one has ever had a bad thing to say about him. Last year was the only exception. His dad had Parkinson's and passed away, and then Eddie went through a divorce. He showed up late frequently and made mistakes, but he's pulled it together since then. He's not a cold-blooded killer."

"They don't wear signs, Laney."

"Check yourself there, Foster." Her tone was level, but there was a hint of anger thrumming through it. "I may not have as many years of investigative experience as you do, but I'm not a rookie. Don't treat me like one."

He deserved that. Jonah blew out a breath. "Yeah. I'm sorry. That was uncalled for."

"So was pushing me out of the way to enter the boathouse first. I'm not helpless."

"No, but there's no way I'm going to let you walk into potential danger first." She opened her mouth to argue, but he shook his head hard. "It's not because you aren't capable. I know you are. But you're also my best friend, and I'm going to keep you safe at all costs. It's who I am, Laney."

Their gazes met, and her expression softened. Jonah realized that what he'd said may have revealed a bit too much, so he booped her on the nose because he knew it would irritate her. "Build a bridge and get over it."

She swatted his hand away. "You're annoying. Why do you always make it so hard to stay mad at you?"

"It's part of my charm."

He was rewarded with a brilliant smile that stole his breath. Laney's chocolate-brown eyes crinkled at the corners as she tried to muster up the energy to continue the argument but couldn't. It was a lost cause anyway. Jonah respected Laney to his core, but he wouldn't apologize for protecting her.

A scream ripped through the air.

EIGHT

Laney's heart jumped into overdrive as she scanned the grassy clearing dotted with oak trees. A little girl, around four years old, lay crumpled on the ground, tears streaking her face. Her knee was bleeding. Laney jogged across the distance between them, Scout at her side, and then crouched down next to the child. "Hi there, sweetheart. My name is Laney, and I'm a park ranger. This is my dog, Scout."

The little girl's pigtails swayed as she lifted her head. Freckles dotted her nose. "I fell while running."

"I see that. You hurt yourself." Laney smiled warmly. "We need to get you inside the visitor center so we can clean up your knee and that scrape on your arm. Do you think you can walk?"

Tears swelled behind sage-green eyes. "I don't think so. It really hurts."

"How about if I carry you?" Jonah bent down. His expression was soft and caring. "Would that be all right?"

She studied him for a moment, her small fingers reaching out to brush the Texas Ranger badge pinned to his shirt. "Are you a police officer? Because my mommy said I can ask for help from police officers."

"Your mommy is a smart lady. And yes, I'm a Texas Ranger, which is a type of police officer."

The little girl beamed and then reached out her hands, showing he could lift her up. Jonah swept her effortlessly into his arms. Laney's heart did a pitter-patter as she watched this side of him emerge. The broad-shouldered lawman with perpetual scowls and grumpy remarks transformed completely by a child's trust. His large hands held the little girl with gentleness, and the tenderness in his blue eyes was captivating. He peppered the child with questions while his long legs ate up the distance to the visitor center.

Alli was indeed four. Her mom's name was Sarah, and she was at the mess hall. They lived in a big house with roses in the garden. She enjoyed camping but didn't want to touch worms while fishing.

Inside the visitor center, Jonah set the little girl down on a chair while Laney fetched the first aid kit from behind the front desk.

Brett had a phone to his ear and said no-comment before hanging up. "The reporters have started calling."

"We knew it would happen." She checked her watch. "The media liaison should be here shortly. Then we can direct all the calls that way." She hurried back to Alli. Scout licked the little girl's hand, eliciting a peal of laughter from her. Laney smiled.

"Alli, I'm gonna go find your mom, while Ranger Torres and Scout bandage up your knee." Jonah nodded toward Laney before hurrying out.

Laney kept up the chatter with Alli while she cleaned her wounds. Both scrapes were minor. She'd just attached a cartoon band-aid to Alli's knee when a woman rushed in. Her red hair—the same shade as Alli's—was pulled back and held by a clip. Worry pinched her features. She was followed by Jonah.

"Sweetie, are you okay?" She bent down beside the child. "What happened?"

"I fell and got a boo-boo."

"You weren't supposed to go this far." She sent an exasperated look in Laney's direction. "I'm so sorry. We were finishing up lunch and a group of kids wanted to play hide and seek. Thank you for helping her."

"It wasn't a problem." She'd worked as a park ranger long enough to know that kids often wandered out of sight. It was part of the adventure of being outdoors, exploring and discovering. As long as they knew how to find help when they needed it, a little independence was healthy.

She smiled at the little girl. "Alli was very brave. And smart enough to tell us your name and where you were. You should be proud of her."

Alli beamed. Laney got down on her level. "Make sure you listen to your mom, okay? Don't go too far, just like she says."

"I will. I promise." Alli hugged Laney and then Scout.

Her mom took her hand. With a wave and a smile, they headed back outside.

Laney collected her first aid kit. "Crisis averted."

Jonah snorted. "If only all our problems were easily fixed with a cartoon bandage."

"Right. Sometimes I miss being a kid." A family had come in while Laney was tending to Alli, and Brett finished assigning them an RV spot. Two school-aged kids ran around in circles, their pent-up energy making Laney suddenly feel old and tired. She hadn't had much sleep last night, and she wished she could bottle their enthusiasm for herself.

She slipped behind the front counter to return the first aid kit as the family exited the building. The silence that followed felt unnatural. Laney knew it wouldn't last, so she took the opportunity to ask, "Brett, what can you tell me about Tyler and Ava? I noticed on their paperwork that you were the one who checked them in."

His expression grew sad. "Yeah. They showed up around 2:30 or so. The check-in itself was uneventful. Tyler booked Campsite 8 when he made the reservation, so there wasn't much to discuss."

Jonah moved closer, his stance casual but his eyes sharp. "How did they seem with each other?"

Brett frowned, his brows furrowing. "To be honest, I didn't really pay that much attention. I'd say fine, I guess." He cast a glance toward Laney. "I'm sorry I don't remember more. People run together, you know? Especially when it's busy."

She knew exactly what he meant. Unless a guest did

something weird, people and conversations blurred together. Brett must've spoken to over fifty people yesterday. "Do you recall if anyone else was in here while Ava and Tyler were checking in? Another guest? Or someone from the staff?"

He tilted his head. "Well, you passed by on your way out to do a patrol. Deputy Ranger Dawson came in, but I don't remember exactly when... Hold on."

Brett drew closer to her, and belatedly, Laney realized he was attempting to get to the computer behind her. She side-stepped as his arm brushed hers. The scent of his cologne hit her. Spicy, familiar, and old-fashioned. Something a thousand men wore. Unbidden, a memory surfaced of her father teaching her to tie fishing knots. Back when he was still Dad. He'd worn the same aftershave.

But beneath that, there was something else. Something darker.

Her breath caught. A flash of darkness overtook her senses, the weight of a body pinning her down, terror filling her chest as she fought for her life—

"Laney. Laney." The voice sounded far away, but then there was pressure on her arm.

She jerked away, accidentally ramming her hip into the corner of the credenza behind the front desk. The papers and plastic shelving vibrated with the force of her movement. A growl erupted from Scout. The sharp sound—along with the pain—cut through her flashback. She blinked to find Brett standing nearby with his hands up in a non-threatening manner. "Whoa. Sorry. Didn't mean to crowd you."

Laney forced a laugh, though her heart was still hammering. "No, you're fine. I think I've had too much coffee today." She pressed a hand to her chest, willing her pulse to slow. "I'm more jittery than I realized."

Jonah was at her side, concern etched on his features. She briefly met his gaze and shook her head. She'd explain to him later about the cologne. Her attacker had worn the same old-fashioned aftershave. But half the men in Texas probably wore it. Her own father had. It was an important detail, and it proved she remembered more about the attack than her mind recalled initially, but it wouldn't lead them directly to the killer.

Scout growled again, the hair on her neck raised. Brett took another step back.

"Scout, heel." Laney's command was sharp. The dog hesitated and then did as she was ordered, although there seemed to be a disgruntled look on her furry face.

Brett eyed her warily. "What's wrong with her? Is she okay?"

Laney laid a hand on Scout's head, rubbing her ears to reassure her. The lab's posture was stiff. She was normally mild-mannered, but she'd been trained to protect her handler. "My quick movements startled her. I think we're both a little on edge after last night's attack."

To put Brett at ease, Laney patted her leg and moved back around to the front of the desk. Scout and Jonah both joined her. She offered a reassuring smile, ignoring the nerves still twisting her stomach. "Sorry about that."

Brett breathed out. "It's okay." He returned her smile, but none of its warmth was reflected in his dark eyes. "I heard Scout was a hero last night. I'm glad you had her to protect you." He bent toward the computer. "I wanted to check my browser history for the time period that Ava and Tyler checked in. Yeah, here we go. 2:45. A guy came in and asked me about obtaining a fishing license. I told him that the camping store should have them, and he wanted to know what time it closed. I had to look it up because Mr. Robbins recently changed the operating hours."

Jonah moved closer to Laney until their shoulders touched. His solid presence was comforting.

"And this guy was here when Ava and Tyler checked in?" Jonah asked.

"Right after. I'm sure he was waiting for me to finish up with Tyler. What made me notice him was how he looked at Ava. It's hard to describe..." Brett squinted off into the distance as if trying to recall the moment. "He stared at her. It struck me as odd."

"Can you describe him?"

"Average height and weight. Maybe in his thirties. Dark hair. A scruffy beard. He was wearing a gray T-shirt and blue jeans."

Jonah asked a few more questions, but Brett couldn't provide further details. Laney could tell he was trying to remember though. She wondered if he was overemphasizing the man's interest in Ava. Brett had always been eager to please. Maybe he was trying too hard to be useful. It was something to keep in mind.

Laney leaned against the counter. "Do you know which campsite he was staying at?"

"He didn't say." Regret pinched his features. "I should've paid more attention. Maybe I'd recognize him if I saw him again, but I can't say for certain. Should I drive around the park after my shift? I'm happy to help in any way I can."

Laney shook her head. Brett wasn't in law enforcement. "No. Looking at Ava doesn't mean he did anything wrong. If the guy comes back into the visitor center or you see him on the park grounds, radio me or Deputy Ranger Dawson. Do not engage with the man yourself." She didn't want Brett—or anyone on her staff—getting hurt. "Do you understand?"

He nodded solemnly. "Yes, ma'am."

Laney held his gaze for a beat, waiting to see if there was any hesitation, but he seemed to take her warning seriously. She relaxed a touch. "Before we go, Brett, we're following standard procedure and checking everyone's whereabouts during the time frame of the murders. Where were you between the hours of seven and midnight yesterday?"

Brett didn't hesitate. "I clocked out at seven and headed into town for the Hill Country Music Festival. Been looking forward to it all week."

"Can I see the tickets?" Jonah asked.

Brett pulled out his phone and showed them a mobile ticket confirmation. "Paid forty bucks for this. The band didn't go on until nine thirty, but I wanted to grab dinner first. Stopped at Rusty's Bar and Grill around seven thirty. Ran into my buddy Jake Whitfield. We had a couple of beers and some wings and watched the game for a bit. Then I headed to the festival around eight forty-five."

"And you were at the festival the rest of the night?" Laney asked.

"Yeah, until about eleven thirty. The place was packed, had to be five thousand people there. Tried to get closer to the stage, but it was wall-to-wall."

Jonah made notes. "Jake can verify you met him at Rusty's?"

"Yeah, for sure. We were there for maybe an hour, hour and fifteen minutes." Brett gave them Jake's number. "Anything else?"

"Not right now," Jonah said, tucking his phone away. His tone was polite, but Laney heard a thread of distrust running through it. "We'll follow up if we need anything else."

Brett's gaze flickered to the bruises encircling Laney's neck before lifting to her face. "I really hope you find whoever did this."

The phone rang before she could respond, and Brett scrambled to answer it. His voice carried across the lobby as Laney and Jonah moved into the hall, heading for her office.

Jonah kept his voice pitched low. "What happened back there?"

She described the flashback. Inside her office, Scout jogged to her bed in the corner and collapsed. Laney popped open the water bottle on her desk and took a long drink. She was still shaken from the memory. "It was intense. And so real...The aftershave isn't a solid clue. It's a popular brand. But clearly, there's more about the assault I remember, even if I can't recall it right now."

"You may get more information in bits and pieces." Jonah placed a hand on her arm. The heat of his touch went straight through the sleeve of her shirt. "Why don't you take a break? I can interview the rest of the employees who were working yesterday."

"No." Laney would not shirk from her responsibility. This was her park. Her staff.

But for how long? The offer to make her position as superintendent, and the decision she faced, hovered in the back of her mind. It was something she didn't have the mental or emotional energy to think about.

Jonah's gaze scanned her face, as physical as a touch. "Are you sure? You're still pale."

"I'm fine." She forced herself to pull away from him and square her shoulders. "I'll get the list of employees who worked yesterday, and we'll question them together."

Jonah studied her for a long moment, then nodded. "All right. But if you need a break—"

"I'll tell you." She managed a small smile. "I promise."

He seemed satisfied with that, pulling out his phone to check his emails. They were waiting on reports from the state lab.

Laney moved to her computer, but her mind kept circling back to that moment in the lobby. The cologne, the flashback, the visceral terror. The aftershave was just one detail. What else had her subconscious locked away? More details about the killer?

Labor Day weekend meant the park was flooded with hundreds of visitors. The thought of a killer moving freely among them made her stomach clench.

They needed answers, and they needed them fast.

NINE

The next morning, Jonah sipped his third cup of coffee while watching the sun rise over the lake. He'd been up since before dawn, patrolling the grounds near Laney's cabin. There were no signs of anyone sneaking around in the woods. At least not today. But that brought him little comfort.

A killer was still out there.

The interviews with rangers and park staff hadn't yielded any suspects. Chief Deputy Williams hadn't had any luck identifying a suspect either after re-interviewing family members and some of Ava and Tyler's friends. Even the lab results had been disappointing.

He was frustrated and broody.

The door to Laney's cabin opened, and Scout bounded out. She beelined for the trees, dipping behind a pine and weaving through bushes. Laney followed. She was dressed for work in her park ranger uniform, but her hair was left free, tumbling over her shoulders in a silky black wave. In one hand, she carried a coffee mug. The smile on her face was soft, and she drew in a deep breath of fresh air before spotting him on the porch next door.

Laney's smile widened, her entire face lighting up. "Morning."

His heart skipped a beat as his breath hitched.

That really needed to stop happening. He'd always harbored romantic feelings for Laney, but until the attack, he'd been able to keep a tight lid on them. "Morning."

"You're scowling." She grinned as she joined him on the porch. Sunlight illuminated the red highlights buried in her hair and the sweep of her cheekbones. "What's the matter? Don't like your coffee?"

He eyed the watered-down brew that supposedly passed for coffee. His cabin was outfitted with a machine that used pods. The result was sorely lacking in his opinion. "It's pathetic."

"Switch with me." She extended her own cup in his direction. "I made mine the way you like it, just in case. I'll drink yours. That way we're both happy."

Warmth washed through him. She'd thought of him. He liked that she thought of him. Too much. And when their fingers brushed as they exchanged cups, his traitorous pulse sped up. Jonah was briefly tempted to take her hand and hold it, but that would've been out of character. They were affectionate with each other. Hugs and brief touches. But always careful. Always friendly.

He sat back in his chair and studied her as she sipped the coffee from his mug. The dark circles under her eyes were gone. She looked fresh-faced. Pretty. "You look better this morning."

"I took a melatonin. Wouldn't have slept otherwise." She kept her focus on the lake as she took another sip of her coffee. "Thanks for keeping watch."

His stomach flipped over. He hadn't told her about his plans. She must've seen him patrolling. The appreciation in her voice did funny things to his insides, even as pride swelled. Laney was as tough as they came. She didn't accept help easily, and despite her sunshine demeanor, trust wasn't something she doled out to everyone. He was among the select few in her inner circle.

Her best friend. It meant everything to him and was a reminder of just how precious their relationship was.

And how easily it could all get screwed up.

Scout jogged up the porch steps, and Jonah smothered her with affection before Laney pulled a ball out of the pocket of her cargo pants. She tossed it, and the lab raced off. Jonah took a drink of the dark brew in his own mug and gave a grunt of approval. "Much better. Thank you."

"You're welcome. I thought we could go into town for breakfast this morning. I know a cute place with the best kolaches in the county." She pushed against the floor, setting her rocking chair into motion. "I figured after that we could regroup. Maybe meet with Chief Deputy Williams to compare notes and see where the investigation stands."

It was a good plan. Jonah was just about to tell her so when his cell phone rang. He pulled it from his pocket, surprised to see Sheriff Morrison was calling. He answered. "Morning, sheriff."

"Morning. Sorry to bother you so early, but Ava's roommate just arrived at my house. She went home to Austin on Thursday for the holiday weekend but drove straight here once she heard the news about..." The sheriff cleared his throat and then pressed on. "Anyway, she has information you're going to want to hear."

Jonah straightened. "Should I call Chief Deputy Williams?"

"Her son is ill, so she needs to take him to the doctor. Normally, I would wait for her, but given the circumstances, I don't think the delay is a good idea."

"Laney and I will be there soon." He hung up and then explained the conversation to Laney. "No time for breakfast."

Thirty minutes later, the sun was blazing as they pulled up to Sheriff Morrison's property. The house was on the small side with a neat front yard and trim hedges. Jonah noted the beat-up Chevy in the driveway. Likely the roommate's. He prayed whatever information the young woman had would lead them straight to the killer.

Laney rang the doorbell. She looked increasingly wilted. Humidity had put a slight curl into her dark locks, and her slacks were wrinkled. She'd left Scout back at the visitor center with Andy. Jonah wiped a bead of sweat from his own brow before settling his cowboy hat back on his head.

A black SUV drifted past on the street, slowing as it passed the house. Tinted windows made it impossible to see the driver. Jonah's gaze tracked it for a moment—probably just a neighbor being nosy about all the law enforcement presence—before the front door swung open.

Grayson had aged fifteen years overnight. Bags hung under his dark eyes, and his olive complexion was ashen. Despite his grief, purpose fueled his movements as he waved them into the foyer. "Thank you for coming. My wife and Ava's parents are at the church meeting with our pastor about..." His jaw hardened, and he swallowed hard as tears filmed his eyes. "The funeral."

"I'm so sorry, sheriff," Laney's tone was comforting and kind. "I can't imagine how difficult this must be for all of you."

He nodded and cleared his throat. "I appreciate that. My brother and sister-in-law are barely functioning. As it is, I'd prefer we get through the interview before they return."

"We'll do the best we can." Jonah couldn't promise anything—not without knowing what Ava's roommate had to say—but he would move heaven and earth to prevent causing this family any more pain. "Would it be better to speak down at the sheriff's department?"

"No. Kylie's pretty distraught, and I don't want to put her through that if it can be avoided." He paused. "She and Ava have been roommates since freshman year. They were very close. Like sisters."

Jonah heard the protective note in Grayson's tone

and respected him for it. The message was clear: treat Kylie gently. She was grieving and fragile, and the sheriff wouldn't tolerate anyone making it worse.

Grayson escorted them into the living room. The space was homey but dated, with paneled walls and over-sized furniture. A petite woman in her early twenties sat tucked in the corner of the couch. Short red curls framed a heart-shaped face and pointed chin. Her eyes were swollen and bloodshot from crying. Sitting next to her, holding her hand, was a thin-faced male with bottle-thick glasses and a goatee.

"Kylie, hon, these are the investigators I told you about." The sheriff's tone was gentle. "Texas Ranger Jonah Foster and Park Ranger Laney Torres." He turned toward Jonah. "This is Kylie Jackson and her boyfriend Parker Wessel."

Jonah gave each of them a nod in greeting before claiming an armchair catercorner to Kylie. Laney hung back, choosing to perch on a recliner near a set of patio doors that led to the backyard. A silent way of letting Jonah take the lead in questioning.

"I'm very sorry for your loss," Jonah started gently. Kylie's lip trembled, and he gave her a moment. "Sheriff Morrison mentioned you and Ava have been roommates for years, and that you have some information about who might've wanted to hurt her." He removed his cell phone from his pocket. "I'd like to record our conversation, if you don't mind. It'll help me recall all the details accurately later."

The young woman nodded, and he hit the record

button, setting the device on the coffee table. Recording the conversation kept his attention on the witness instead of on taking notes, which meant his sole attention was on whatever Kylie had to say.

Jonah offered an encouraging look. "When was the last time you spoke to Ava?"

"On Thursday afternoon, when she left for the camping trip. Tyler planned the whole thing for their three-year anniversary, and she... she..." Kylie glanced at her boyfriend, tears welling in her eyes.

Parker scooted closer on the couch and ran his thumb over the back of her hand. "Ava suspected Tyler was going to propose on the trip. Kylie had the difficult task of convincing her that Ty was just being sweet, and that he hadn't so much as hinted at proposing, but Ava didn't seem convinced."

"I'm not a good liar." Kylie gave Jonah a watery smile. "Ty had been planning everything for months. He was going to propose on Sunday, out on the water, at their favorite swimming spot. It was the first place he'd told Ava he loved her."

Jonah felt a stab of grief for the couple. Their young lives had been cut far too short, and learning they were in love and on the cusp of getting engaged made their deaths all the more awful. He'd worked countless murders, but there were a few that buried deep in his heart. This was turning out to be one of them.

It took several seconds to box his emotions up tight. Judging from the way Laney pressed her lips together, she struggled to keep her sadness in check as well. Jonah would never have wished this experience on his best friend, but somehow, in some inexplicable way, he felt comforted knowing she shared his heartbreak.

He focused back on Kylie. "So their relationship was going well then."

"They only had eyes for each other." Her jaw tightened along with her posture. "But Ava attracted attention from other guys. She was gorgeous and had this carefree way about her... she never encouraged anyone. Not once. But she was asked out a lot whenever Ty wasn't around."

He heard what she was hesitant to say. Jonah glanced at the sheriff, whose expression was guarded. Although he'd already heard this information, Grayson was bracing himself for what would come next. Controlled anger. That was how Jonah would describe him.

It sparked a concern that Grayson would take matters into his own hands, but he quashed those concerns. The sheriff had called him. He'd done this by the book and was trusting that Jonah would see it through. The weight of that trust and responsibility added another boulder to the sack of pressures on his back. Finding the killer wouldn't bring back Ava and Tyler, but it was all Jonah could do to ease the family's grief and pain.

He refocused his attention back on Kylie. "Was there someone in particular who was interested in Ava?"

"Yes. Ava majored in Forestry, and during the spring semester, she took a class from a visiting lecturer about Outdoor Recreation Management. She was excited because it meant learning all the trails in Piney Woods State Park. It was her intention to get a summer job there as a camping guide, especially since she'd had such a great time volunteering the year before."

Laney leaned forward. "Ava was a volunteer for the park? In what area?"

"She handled wildlife programs for school groups," Grayson answered. "She volunteered there only a few times a year. Between her classes and the part-time job at the university, which helped pay her tuition, Ava didn't have much free time."

Laney nodded. "We have hundreds of volunteers cycling through, especially for educational programs. I wish I could say I remember her, but..." She trailed off, frustration evident in the tight line of her mouth.

Jonah waited a moment in case she had a follow-up question, but when she didn't speak, he returned the focus back to the matter at hand. "You mentioned someone was interested in Ava."

"It was her professor," Kylie declared. "His name is Garrett Wheeler. He runs a tour guide business called Texas Camping and Trail Guides."

The name meant nothing to Jonah, but from the way Grayson and Laney stiffened, they were both familiar with Garrett. The man must be a local. Or at least knowledgeable enough about the Piney Woods trail system to teach a university class on it.

Jonah leaned forward. This could be the break they needed in the case. "What happened between Ava and Garrett?"

"About three weeks after class started, Garrett asked Ava to hang back under the pretense of discussing a paper she'd written. He flirted with her, and it made Ava very uncomfortable. She told him she had a boyfriend, hoping he would get the hint. But he didn't care. Garrett kept finding ways to be alone with her, or he flirted with her in class. Eventually, he asked her out, and she once again explained that she had a boyfriend." Kylie's mouth flattened. "His response was that Ty didn't have to know anything. They could keep it a secret."

Jonah's gut clenched. He'd met men like Garrett before. Guys who didn't believe in listening to no, who thought that every woman was simply playing hard to get. Had Garrett's interest in Ava slipped into an obsession? Had he become angry enough with her rejection to kill her?

"How did Ava respond?" Jonah asked.

"She told him there was no way she would ever cheat on Ty." Kylie blew out a breath. "I urged her to report Garrett to the university, but she was worried about creating a fuss with only a few weeks left in the class. As far as I know, Garrett left her alone after that, but Ava was uncomfortable enough around him she decided not to take a job at Piney Woods for the summer. She didn't want to constantly run into him."

Jonah couldn't fault Ava for being reluctant to start a formal inquiry into the matter, but Garrett's actions bordered on harassment. At the very least, they were morally reprehensible. "Did Ava tell Tyler about what was going on?"

"A bit. Tyler wasn't the jealous kind, but he was protective." Kylie looked at her boyfriend.

Parker took her hand. "Tyler would've approached Garrett and had it out with him. With the little that Ava had told him, he was ready to do just that, but she begged him to stay out of it. Against his better judgment, Tyler agreed." He sighed. "If he'd known the entire story—especially about Garrett finding ways to be alone with Ava—he would've interceded."

Jonah turned toward the sheriff. "I assume you didn't know about this either?"

Grayson shook his head, his expression hard. "She didn't breathe a word of it to me. Probably for the same reason she didn't tell Tyler. Ava knew I would push her to press charges and get the university involved."

"Was Ava living in town over the summer? Did she have any additional interactions with Garrett after the class was over?"

Kylie hesitated. "She and Tyler worked at Big Bend National Park over the summer. They just came back two weeks ago. Ava mentioned seeing Garrett in an ice cream shop last week while on a date with Tyler. He didn't talk to her, but I could tell she was uncomfortable about it."

"Did she explain why?"

"No, it was just a feeling I had." Kylie's eyes welled with fresh tears. "I should've demanded she tell the university about what was going on. Or when she saw him, I should've forced her to call her uncle." Her gaze shot to Grayson. "I'm so sorry..."

She burst into tears. Parker appeared helpless in the

face of her grief. Grayson crossed the room and bent in front of her, gathering her into his arms in a fatherly hug. "This is not your fault. You hear me? No one blames you."

Their pain was raw and heartbreaking to witness.

Jonah caught Laney's eye and tilted his head toward the door. They'd gotten what they needed, and staying would only prolong Kylie's pain. He reached for his phone on the coffee table to stop the recording. "Thank you for speaking with us, Kylie. I know how difficult this is."

She nodded against Grayson's shoulder, unable to respond.

They saw themselves out and, within moments, were driving through the neighborhood.

Jonah adjusted the vent, letting the blast of air-conditioning wash over his face. Then he reached for his laptop tucked under the passenger-side seat. He did a quick background check on Garrett Wheeler. "Guy's clean. No arrest record. He has a speeding ticket from three years ago, but that's it." He glanced at Laney. Her focus was on the road. "What do you know about Garrett?"

"He's a local, and his business is successful." Laney's hands tightened on the steering wheel. "But there are rumors. Shortly after joining the staff at Piney Woods, three separate women on different occasions told me Garrett is a player, and I should steer clear."

Jonah's gut clenched. "Has he ever hit on you?"

She shot him a feral smile. "No. I'm too... up front for

someone like Garrett. He likes his woman demure and reserved." Her expression faded into a pained one. "Someone like Ava, a woman working hard to get through college and unwilling to pursue charges, is just the kind of victim he'd zero in on. He flirted with her to test the waters, and when she didn't threaten to turn him in to the university, he pushed harder."

"You make him sound like a predator?" His gaze narrowed. "What exactly did the other women—the ones who warned you about Garrett—say?"

"Just that I should be careful. It wasn't so much what they said... it was more of a feeling. Like he'd made them uncomfortable." She flipped on her blinker. "You hear something once, you dismiss it. But three different women on three different occasions..." Laney shook her head. "I've also observed him flirting with staff members and volunteers."

Jonah was about to ask another question, but the words died on his lips when he caught sight of a black SUV in the side-view mirror. It was two cars back. Tinted windows.

The same vehicle that had slowly passed Morrison's house.

"I assume you want to interview Garrett?" Laney asked. "He works on Saturdays, so he's at his office or at the park. I think we should try the office first."

"Yeah." He never took his eyes off the SUV. Sunlight glinted off the windshield, making it impossible to see the driver, and the license plate was hidden by the cars separating them.

Laney made a turn onto Main Street, and the SUV followed. They drove past neat shops with wide awnings on tree-lined streets. The vehicle hung back but made another turn behind them a few moments later.

Jonah's pulse kicked up. They were being followed.

TEN

Laney rolled to a stop at a red light and forced her fingers to loosen their grip on the steering wheel. Her insides were in knots, her mind turning over everything they'd learned from Kylie. As a camping and trail guide, Garrett Wheeler knew every inch of Piney Woods. Probably better than she did.

Part of her wanted it to be him. Needed it to be him.

Not because she had anything personal against Garrett—though she'd never liked the man—but because if Garrett was the killer, at least it made sense. A predator who harassed women, who wouldn't take no for an answer, who saw Ava as a conquest he'd been denied. That was a motive she could understand. A suspect she could stomach.

The alternative was worse. That the killer was someone else. She'd seen evil up close during her military service, had been in its presence, but that was different.

This time, the killer was from her community. Someone she knew and trusted. Someone she'd laughed with over coffee or worked alongside on search and rescue operations.

It caused goosebumps to skitter across her skin.

"I think we're being followed." Jonah's tone was clipped, his attention fixed on the side-view mirror. "Black SUV. Two cars back. It's been mirroring our movements through town."

Her eyes shot to the rearview mirror. She spotted the SUV but couldn't see the driver. "It would be foolish for the killer to follow us. Maybe it's just someone heading in the same direction as we are."

"Possibly." He spared her a look. "But don't underestimate this perpetrator, Laney. He committed cold-blooded murder, attacked you, and then hid in the woods near your cabin yesterday morning." He stared at the vehicle in the side-view mirror. "Whoever this is, he's bold. He also may be running scared, worried about what we'll uncover. Or what you'll remember."

Laney had to admit Jonah had a point. She ran through possible options as the light changed to green. Pulling into the intersection, she kept her pace steady. The streets were full of Saturday traffic as people ran errands. A farm truck loaded down with hay passed them.

She took a sudden left onto a quieter side street without using her blinker and followed it with a quick right. A few seconds later, the SUV appeared behind them. The driver still wasn't visible, and a dark-tinted cover obscured the license plate, making it impossible to read from this distance.

"Okay, I think you're right. He's following us." She calculated her options and then hit the gas. "Hold on." Laney sailed through a yellow light and then made a sudden U-turn in the wide intersection, now heading directly toward the SUV. "Let's get a look at this guy."

But the driver counter-maneuvered by running a red light, nearly clipping a Toyota in the process, and taking a sharp left turn into a neighborhood. Laney flipped on her lights while hitting the gas, just as a garbage truck turned onto the road. Frustration built as she lost valuable seconds going around the large vehicle before turning onto the residential street in pursuit.

The SUV was nowhere to be seen.

Laney slowed, keeping her eyes peeled for the SUV and watching for pedestrians or kids on bicycles. "Any sign of him?"

"No." Jonah's gaze scanned each turnoff as they passed it. The furrow on his brow deepened. "He could be anywhere. For all we know, he lives in this neighborhood, and the SUV is tucked up in his garage." He blew out a breath before tossing her a smile. "Nice try though."

His praise took the edge off her frustration, and she grinned back. But something else stirred beneath the surface. It'd been happening more and more lately. A quickening of her heartbeat when he looked at her like that. The awareness of his presence beside her felt different than it used to.

She'd noticed it after Breanna's wedding. It bothered

her... this interfering attraction. She'd done her best to wrangle it under control, taking it as a sign that maybe it was time to think about having a relationship that lasted over six weeks.

So she'd tried to date Mike. Disaster. Oh, he'd been a really nice guy. So nice that she'd felt horrible... like she was leading him on. Because dating him hadn't diminished this new awareness of Jonah at all. Breaking up had been a relief. The busy summer—and the extra responsibilities—had limited her time with Jonah. She'd almost fooled herself into thinking that everything was back to normal.

And then the attack happened. The sound of his voice on the phone, rough with worry. The way he'd shown up, the protective way he'd reacted, the way he'd held her and so casually kissed the top of her head. It'd awakened something she hadn't even realized was there, a longing she didn't know how to name and wasn't sure she wanted to.

Because wanting Jonah that way? It was a surefire way to lose him.

So she forced a smile and a lightness to her voice to hide the irritating and irrational butterflies fluttering in her stomach. "Was that a compliment? And a smile? Careful, Foster. People might not recognize you without your trademark scowl."

He grunted in reply, which only made her grin widen. She enjoyed teasing him. It was familiar ground.

And right now, she needed familiar.

Her stomach rumbled. They'd skipped breakfast.

"The kolache place isn't far. Let's grab some food on our way to interview Garrett."

His brow rose. "Coffee?"

She bounced in her seat at the thought of an iced latte. "I know just the place."

Twenty minutes later, fortified with food and caffeine, she crossed the parking lot of the strip mall toward Texas Camping and Trail Guides. Her gaze scanned the vehicles. Garrett's blue pickup truck, with its distinctive rock-climbing stickers on the bumper, sat a short distance away. There were no other vehicles registered either to him or to his business. Jonah had checked.

So where would Garrett have gotten a black SUV? The thought nagged at her as she crossed the threshold into a cold blast of air-conditioning. A glass-topped counter dominated the front area, filled with compasses, multi-tools, and expensive GPS devices. Brochures fanned across the surface, promising authentic adventures and guided backpacking experiences.

Laney approached the unmanned front desk and tapped the silver service bell. Its cheerful ding echoed through the narrow space. Jonah leaned against the counter, studying the wide array of knives inside, his scowl on full display.

"Be right there!" Garrett's voice called from somewhere in the back, followed by the sound of a chair scraping against the floor and heavy footsteps on hardwood. Moments later, he appeared. Five-eight, with a bulky physique that came from bench pressing weights and regular rock climbing, Garrett Wheeler moved with the deliberate confidence of someone used to being in charge. His moisture-wicking shirt and utility pants looked expensive but practical. Messy dark hair gave him an easygoing appearance, supported by the well-worn hiking boots and a quick smile. That grin tempered just a touch when his gaze landed on Laney before shifting to Jonah and flickering back again.

"Hi, Garrett." She offered him a reassuring smile. "Sorry to pop in unannounced, but we need to speak to you about an important matter." Laney gestured toward Jonah and introduced him. "We're investigating the murder of a couple killed at the park yesterday."

"I heard about that. Really tragic." Garrett's gaze lifted as Jonah stood to his full height, all six foot four inches, and something flickered in his eyes. Wariness, maybe? Or calculation? Whatever it was, he smoothed it over with a handshake before checking his watch. "I have a client meeting in fifteen minutes—"

"It won't take long." Laney wouldn't let him weasel out of answering their questions, if she could help it. Using Jonah's tactic, she removed her cell phone from her pocket. "Do you mind if I record this conversation? It'll help with my report later."

Garrett's expression shifted from evasive to full-on irritation. "Actually, I do mind." He crossed his arms over his broad chest, puffing it up to make it even bigger. His eyes locked on hers. "What's this all about, Laney?"

His tone bordered on hostile, but she didn't let an ounce of annoyance creep into her words. She kept her voice light and friendly. "We're speaking to anyone who might've known the victims, and since you run one of the most popular camping and trail guiding companies, it seemed likely they'd used your services before. Did you know Ava Morrison or Tyler Chen?"

He hesitated. Laney could practically see the wheels in his head turning as Garrett calculated what answer to give them. Finally, he puffed out some air. "I knew Ava. Not well, mind you. She was a student in a class I taught at the university this past spring."

Okay. One point for being honest, although she noted that he tried to downplay his interaction with Ava. "What did you think of her?"

"She was a good student. Conscientious, almost to the point of perfectionism. If I remember right, she got an A in the class."

"Did you interact with her outside of class?"

"Of course not." His eyes tracked Jonah as he crossed the room and helped himself to some water from the cooler. "That would be against the university's policy."

"Huh." She let some confusion enter her tone as her brow furrowed. "That's strange. We interviewed some of Ava's friends, and they told us you interacted with Ava outside of class." There was no law against the police lying to a suspect, so she kept the information vague. If Garrett was the killer, Laney didn't want to give him a reason to go after Kylie. "In fact, we were told that you flirted with Ava and asked her out several times."

Garrett froze and then his jaw tightened, a muscle along his cheek pulsing as he clenched his teeth. He glowered down at her. "This is feeling more like an inter-rogation. Do I need a lawyer?"

She frowned slightly and shrugged. "I don't know. Do you?" She leaned against the counter, keeping her posture casual. "Listen, we can take you down to the sheriff's department, put you in an interview room, let you call your lawyer, wait for him or her to arrive, and then continue this conversation. I have no issues with that. But," she dragged out the word to make a point, "it'll mess up your entire day. And honestly, it's not much fun for me either. Or we could just have a friendly chat right here and clear things up now."

Garrett seemed to consider her words. She couldn't tell if he was nervous because he was tangled up in the murder or if he was simply worried about ruining future opportunities with the university. People hid things for all kinds of reasons.

Laney smiled disarmingly. "We're not interested in going after you for breaking university policy. We're looking for a killer. The sooner we get this over with, the faster we can all go about our business."

Garrett blew out a breath, and his shoulders dropped. "Okay, look, Ava and I flirted. She was gorgeous and smart, and we shared a love of the outdoors. We hit it off immediately. I knew it was against the university's rules, but I figured it was harmless." He mirrored Laney's body language, leaning against the counter. "I mean, come on. We're all adults, you know what I mean?"

"Of course." She tipped closer conspiratorially. "Sometimes workplaces have the stupidest rules."

"Don't they?" Appreciation shimmered in his dark eyes.

"So, did you and Ava ever go out on a date? Or was it just flirting?"

"That's the thing. I wanted to wait until the class was over, but she kept hinting more and more about going out, so finally, I asked her. That's when she told me about her boyfriend."

"The news surprised you?"

"A little, but if I'm being honest," Garrett's grin was quick and cocky, "I've found that relationship labels mean different things to people. Who am I to judge? I figured Ava was just letting me know so I wouldn't expect anything serious. Better for me, you know? I like to keep things light and fun."

"Makes sense. Why tie yourself down to just one person?"

"Exactly." He tilted his head, shifting closer until his arm was nearly brushing hers. The scent of his cologne—something musky and dark—overpowered her senses. It took everything in Laney not to recoil. "I'm usually an excellent judge of character, but you're surprising me, Laney. I always figured you were uptight, but I'm thinking I was wrong about you."

Oh, for heaven's sake. Laney caught herself before she rolled her eyes. Instead, she pasted on an encouraging, borderline flirty smile, and said, "So what happened after Ava told you about her boyfriend? Did y'all go out?"

"No, that's the weird thing. Ava started avoiding me

after that. I took the hint and left her alone. Plenty of other women I can date."

"That's interesting," Laney said carefully. "Because the way we heard it, you were the one pursuing her. Finding ways to be alone with her."

Garrett's expression darkened. "I don't know who told you that, but they're lying."

"So you're saying Ava was the one who came on to you?" Laney kept her tone neutral, but she watched his reaction closely.

"I'm saying whoever told you that story has it backwards. Yeah, I flirted with her. I already admitted that. But I wasn't some creep stalking her around campus." His jaw tightened. "Look, I don't know what people are saying about me, but I didn't do anything wrong."

Jonah scoffed from his section of the office. "Oh, please. Are we supposed to believe that?" He crushed the plastic cup in his hand and shot it across the room into the trash bin. "You pursued Ava even though it was against the rules, you made her uncomfortable by inappropriately flirting with her, then you asked her out, and when she said no, you got your feelings hurt and did something about it."

Jonah planted his hands on his hips and glowered down at Garrett. "Laney might buy this story you're trying to push, but I don't."

"Is this guy for real?" Garrett asked Laney before straightening up to his full height. He tried to look intimidating, puffing out his chest, but against Jonah's imposing frame—eight inches taller and built like he could bench press a truck—Garrett's stocky build came across as compact rather than commanding. "I don't like your tone or your accusations."

Jonah flashed a biting smile. "I don't much care if you like my tone. As far as accusations go, I haven't made one yet. Where were you between the hours of seven and midnight on Thursday night?"

Garrett's cheeks heated as he took an aggressive step toward Jonah. "I don't answer to you."

Laney planted herself between the two men. "Enough. Jonah, cool it. Garrett is trying to help us." She'd seen Jonah interrogate suspects before, but something about watching him now—protective and fierce—made her pulse quicken in a way that had nothing to do with professional admiration.

She turned back to face Garrett. His attention was still locked on Jonah, anger pouring off him, as potent as his cologne. The man had a temper all right. He was also roughly the same height and weight as her attacker, although that didn't mean much. Her description couldn't be relied upon. Everything had happened so quickly.

"No one is accusing you of anything." Laney placed a hand on Garrett's bicep. The move had the desired effect of bringing his focus back to her. "But it would help to know where you were last night. We're asking everyone the same question. It's routine."

His mouth flattened into a thin line. "I was with friends. A buddy of mine is visiting from Utah with his fiancée. They're in town for the music festival. They're staying at the park, in Cabin 3. I arrived around seven with dinner from that BBQ place down the street, and then we hung out and had some drinks. Left around midnight." His eyes searched hers. "I had nothing to do with these murders. Ava... yes, I liked her, but I'm not in the habit of chasing someone who isn't interested. Why would I? There are plenty of other women to date."

He'd lost the cocky attitude, and his tone was so forthright, Laney could almost believe he was telling the truth.

Almost.

But not quite.

"We'll need to verify your alibi," Jonah said flatly. "Names and contact information for your friends in Cabin 3."

Garrett's jaw tightened, but he pulled out his phone. "Fine. Hold on." He scrolled for a moment before rattling off the information. "Nolan Carlson and his fiancée, Lisa Valdez. Nolan's been my friend since high school. He'll tell you I was there until midnight."

"Did you interact with anyone else?" Laney asked. "Another camper, maybe?"

He shook his head. "No."

Too bad. It would've been nice to have an independent person verify Garrett's whereabouts. Laney didn't trust him. She'd sensed he'd lied during their interview, and he was the kind of guy who'd have a friend cover for him.

They headed back to the truck in silence. Laney's mind churned through the interview, trying to separate what felt true from what felt like manipulation. Garrett was hiding something. But was it murder, or just his predatory behavior toward women?

She hopped into the front seat. The A/C pouring from the vents was tepid when she fired up the engine.

Jonah slid into the passenger seat. His body moved with a powerful grace that was riveting. She found herself staring, noting the curve of his jaw, the way his lower lip was a bit fuller than the top one, and the thickness of his hand as he adjusted the air vent. "What do you think?"

She blinked. "What?"

"About Garrett?" He turned to face her, and his brow creased. Confusion flickered in his eyes as he touched his chin. "What is it? Do I have something on my face?"

"No." Her cheeks heated, and she busied herself with buckling her seat belt. "Uh, I think Garrett's a sleaze. He's manipulative, and I don't buy that Ava came on to him. But... I'm not sure he's a killer. He doesn't seem quite controlled enough to carry out a complicated murder. You?"

Jonah didn't answer at first. She peeked at him out of the corner of her eye. He was staring at her with a strange look, as if he was trying to figure out a puzzle while holding the wrong piece in his hand. She put the SUV in gear and backed out of the spot, far too aware of the deepening blush on her cheeks. Focusing on the case was the only way to escape the embarrassment, so she asked again, "What do you think of Garrett?"

"I dunno." Jonah scowled as he glanced back at

Garrett's business. "You're right that he's a hothead, but he's also sneaky. He tried to downplay knowing Ava at first. And he definitely isn't one to take no for an answer. I could easily see him getting mad that she rejected him and wanting revenge."

Laney turned, steering them toward the park. "Let's talk to Nolan and Lisa, see if Garrett's alibi holds up."

Jonah removed a package of breath mints from his pocket and popped one in his mouth before offering the tin to her. "Think they'll tell us the truth?"

"Only one way to find out."

ELEVEN

The heat beat down on Jonah's shoulders as he watched kids use a rope swing to jump into the lake. The screams of enjoyment carried up the hill. Hamburgers sizzled on a nearby grill. A group of parents kept watch over the kids swimming while preparing dinner.

Inside the visitor center, Laney was checking Nolan and Lisa's reservation. Jonah had almost gone with her, but he'd needed a moment.

To cool his head. To think.

Watching Garrett Wheeler practically drool over Laney had been hard. It'd taken every ounce of his self-control and training to stay next to the cooler, when what he'd really wanted to do was get that creep away from her. At the same time, he'd been proud. She'd handled the interview like a pro. Her flirty smile hadn't been genuine, but no one other than him would've noticed.

His mind had been on Garrett and the case, which is why he'd been thrown off when he'd caught her staring at him in the car. The way her eyes skittered away from his, the blush on her cheeks... if he didn't know better, Jonah would've thought she'd been checking him out.

But that was ridiculous. Laney had made it clear fifteen years ago that they didn't work as a couple. She'd broken up with him, kindly but firmly, and they'd built something better—a friendship that had lasted through jobs, moves, relationships, and everything else life threw at them.

Laney hadn't shown a shred of romantic interest in him for a very long time.

So why had she been staring?

Someone called out his name. Jonah turned to find Texas Ranger Ryker Montgomery strolling toward him. A new cowboy hat shielded his eyes from the sun, and the belt buckle at his waist gleamed. He looked well-rested and tanned from spending two weeks in Hawaii. Jonah met him halfway. "So you came back after all. We were taking bets on whether you would."

"I almost didn't." Ryker grinned, his eyes crinkling at the corners. "If I thought for one second I could convince Hannah to live on the beach with me, I'd do it. Clear skies, blue waters, my wife in a bathing suit—"

"Stop, dude." Jonah thought of Hannah like a sister. He scowled. "Not okay. Just... no."

Ryker chuckled. His happiness was palpable. It was getting harder and harder to be in Company A. The rangers were marrying left and right. Ryker and Hannah deserved every happiness in the world, but hearing about it sent a weird pang of longing through Jonah. He wanted that. A wife. A family. But no one had ever come close to claiming his heart.

No one but Laney.

And that was a nonstarter.

The door to the visitor center opened, and Laney emerged, Scout trotting behind her. The dog's tail wagged, and she raced ahead to greet Jonah. He stroked her soft ears only to have her abandon him for Ryker, who gave her a good rubdown.

Laney's smile was breathtakingly sweet. "Well, look at who's back from his honeymoon." Ryker abandoned Scout to give Laney a brotherly hug. She leaned back and stared at him for a moment. "Marriage looks good on you, Ryker. You're happy."

"Hannah makes it easy. Thanks for the crockpot and the cookbooks, by the way. It was one of our favorite wedding gifts. We can't wait to make chili."

"It's the best gift for busy people." She slipped an arm through Jonah's. The casual touch shouldn't have made his pulse skip—she did it often—but somehow his heart couldn't quite get in sync with his head. "And I can't take all the credit. Jonah picked out the cookbooks himself. We spent an hour in the bookstore. I think he looked through every single book in the cooking section."

Ryker's brows shot up. "Impossible. Jonah doesn't cook."

He scowled. "Actually, I do. I use a crockpot all the time."

It'd been a gift from Laney. Truth be told, the wedding gift for Ryker and Hannah had been her idea too. But that was the thing about Laney. She never over-looked his contribution. No matter how small, no matter how seemingly insignificant... she noticed. She *saw* him. Growing up in a family where he'd never fit in, never felt good enough, her easy recognition was a balm on those scarred wounds.

A light breeze ruffled the strands of Laney's hair, and the clean smell of her soap tickled his nose. Jonah, stupidly, breathed in deep. Ryker's gaze narrowed slightly, and a smirk played on his lips. Jonah shot his friend a dirty look. He'd been fending off commentary from his fellow rangers—and their significant others—about his relationship with Laney for years. "Where's Tate?"

"He should be here any minute." Ryker checked his watch. "He was ten minutes behind me, but you know Tate. He drives like a grandma."

"What's that about my driving?" Texas Ranger Tate Atwood came around the side of the building. His curly black hair was cropped military short and matched his rigid bearing. He had the athletic build of someone who played sports naturally, but the guarded look of the quiet kid always chosen last for the team.

As the newest member of Company A, Jonah hadn't worked with Tate much, but he'd found him detailed. The two men couldn't be more different. Ryker was all charm and personality, a touch loud, but with determined dedication that made him pursue cases long after others gave up. Tate was reserved and rarely cracked a joke. He wasn't unfriendly... just measured.

"I said you drive like a grandma." Ryker lightly shoved Tate in greeting. "'Bout time you showed up. I thought we'd have to send out a few patrols to find you."

"You're hilarious." Tate's smile said he didn't mind the joke. But he didn't poke back at Ryker. That was something Jonah noticed. He could take the ribbing without an issue but never dished it back.

Jonah had no such reservations. He snorted. "I'd rather ride with Tate than you. Last time I was in a car with Ryker, he changed lanes three times in five seconds while eating a breakfast taco and arguing with Hannah on speakerphone. Nearly took out a semi."

Everyone laughed. Even Tate's mouth quirked.

"In my defense," Ryker said, grinning, "Hannah was wrong about which exit we needed, and the taco was delicious."

"You're a menace," Laney said, shaking her head. But her smile was fond.

The laughter faded naturally, and Ryker's expression sobered. "So. Two victims, attacked at their campsite. What are we looking at?"

Jonah appreciated the shift. As much as he valued his friendships with these men, they had work to do. "Let's go inside and I'll fill you in on where we're at."

The group trekked inside. Their boots were loud against the lobby's tile floor. Jonah noted Brett wasn't working today. A young brunette was behind the counter. She waved to Laney, but her eyes looked worried as she took in the group of Texas Rangers. Jonah offered her a reassuring smile. They could've set up the task force in the sheriff's department, but it seemed easier to stay on site in the park. It also allowed Jonah to stick close to Laney. He didn't like the idea of her being alone, even if she was a fellow law enforcement officer. Especially not being followed.

Laney led them to a conference room. "You guys can use this as your headquarters for the time being. There's a break room across the hall stocked with coffee and snacks. Help yourself." She took a deep breath. "I really appreciate you guys being here. It means a lot."

"Don't think twice about it." Ryker squeezed her arm as he passed by to grab a seat at the head of the table. He set his backpack down and pulled out a laptop.

Tate followed suit, grabbing a chair and one of the bottled waters in the center while his computer booted up. He slung his messenger bag over the back of the chair. "What can you tell us?"

Jonah ran through everything as succinctly as possible. He pushed the binder he'd been compiling into the center of the table. "The lab reports are here, but I can tell you they haven't found anything helpful so far. Our primary suspect at the moment is Garrett Wheeler. He was a guest lecturer at the university Ava attended, and according to her roommate, harassed Ava." He detailed what Kylie had said, along with their interview with Garrett. "He claims to have an alibi. Laney and I were just about to check it out when you arrived."

"What kind of alibi?" Tate asked, looking up from his keyboard. His fingers had been flying while Jonah was talking. Tate always took detailed notes.

"He says he was with friends staying in Cabin 3," Laney offered. She checked her phone. "According to our records, the cabin was rented by Nolan Carlson for a week. He's due to check out on Wednesday."

"If Nolan verifies Garrett's alibi, then this case goes back to square one," Jonah added. "Laney and I interviewed everyone working at the park on the day of the murders. The front desk clerk, Brett Harrison, mentioned seeing a man looking at Ava in the lobby, but he couldn't give a good description of him. And I can't be certain he wasn't embellishing the story. But it's something we should follow up on. We should also run background checks on all the employees. Rangers are done every year, but administrative employees are only every five years." He pushed a list toward Tate. "Start with these. These people were working on the day of the murder. Then we'll go backward from there."

"Got it." Tate pulled the list closer.

"Why don't you and Laney go talk to Nolan?" Ryker suggested. "That'll give me time to go through the crime scene photos and lab reports. We can reconvene back here and discuss the next steps. Our priorities may change depending on what Nolan says."

He had a point. Jonah nodded. "Sounds like a plan. We'll be back soon."

Scout followed them out of the conference room and into the bright sunshine. Jonah scanned the area, looking for any sign of trouble, as he pulled his sunglasses out of the front pocket of his shirt. The shouts of the kids still swimming rose from the lake. Relief uncoiled the knots in his stomach. He felt lighter having his fellow rangers here. Like the weight bearing down on his shoulders wasn't so heavy.

As they crossed the parking lot to her car, Jonah popped a peppermint in his mouth before offering one to Laney.

She plucked the small, round breath mint out of the tin with a smile. "Every time we hang out, I get hooked on these. Then I always forget to buy some for myself when I'm at the store."

"I'll stock your pantry with them."

She laughed. Laney loaded Scout up, and a few minutes later, they were driving toward Cabin 3. The road was lined with tall pines. A squirrel jumped in front of her vehicle, and she slowed to let the small animal pass. "Have you ever worked a case with Tate before?"

"Once or twice. Why?"

She shrugged. "He's very... tall, dark, and silent." Laney shot him a teasing look. "I didn't think anyone was less talkative than you. Just goes to show, never say never."

A pinch of jealousy grabbed hold of Jonah. "He's single, if that's what you're getting at." The words came out clipped and with more of a scowl than he'd intended.

Her nose wrinkled, and she shot him a look that indicated he was being foolish. "I wasn't."

Heat crawled up the back of his neck. What was wrong with him? Laney had made an innocent observation about Tate's personality, and he'd jumped to jealousy like some territorial teenager. He needed to get his head straight. "Sorry. It's been a long day."

"You didn't sleep much last night, and it's been a while since we had kolaches and coffee." Laney wiggled her eyebrows at him. "How about we stop by the mess hall for dinner? I heard a rumor that lasagna was on the menu."

"Again, I'm not some troll you have to throw food and caffeine at every once in a while. I'm allowed to be in a bad mood. We're getting nowhere fast on a double homicide."

"It hasn't been the first time you've dealt with a tough case. Just admit it, Jonah. Life is better with food, coffee, and sleep. Maybe not in that order, but you get my drift." She beamed and reached across to jab a finger in his midsection. "Admit it. Come on. You can say I'm right."

He jerked away from her. "Absolutely not." But Jonah couldn't stop a smile from forming at the corners of his mouth. Truth was, she was right. He operated better with food, sleep, and caffeine. Most people did. Laney was one of the few individuals he knew who could be starving and still be positive.

She turned onto a dirt road, and Cabin 3 appeared. The rustic log structure hunched between towering pines, their branches creaking softly in the late-afternoon breeze. Cicadas droned from the underbrush, and the air hung heavy with the scent of pine needles and approaching twilight. Jonah felt uneasy as he approached the front door. "No lights on inside. They may not be here."

"The air-conditioning unit is running," Laney pointed out. "But you're right. There's no sign of their vehicle."

He opened the screen door and knocked on the wooden one. No answer. He waited a moment and then tried again to be sure. Logically, Jonah knew the lack of a response was likely because no one was inside, but his skin prickled with apprehension. He let the screen door slam shut.

"What is it?" Laney asked.

"I'm not sure." He scanned the cabin and the surroundings, trying to pinpoint what had set off his internal alarm bells. The hum of the air conditioner mixed with the chirp of the cicadas. Dark shadows deepened between the trees.

Laney laid a hand on his arm. "Something's wrong."

She pointed to Scout. The lab hung back, away from the door. Jonah could've sworn there was a mournful look on her furry face. His pulse skipped a beat. Giving in to his instincts, and Scout's, he circled the small cabin. At each window, he peered inside. Everything appeared normal. Dishes in the kitchen sink, a checkers game on the coffee table, a throw blanket unfolded and dumped in a heap on the couch. Jonah used the light from his flashlight to peer down the hall to the bedroom.

And his breath caught.

A bloody handprint stained the wall.

TWELVE

Two more murders. And a killer still at large.

Jonah stood at the front of the conference room while members of the task force claimed seats. Across the room, from the far end of the oval table, Laney met his gaze. Her park ranger uniform was perfectly pressed, but the dark smudges under her eyes showed she hadn't slept any better than he had. Since finding the bodies yesterday, it'd been a hectic 24 hours. Scout, her ever-trusted companion, lay on the floor at her feet.

Laney offered him a small, encouraging smile. She knew he hated being the center of attention, and somehow, that gesture reached inside his chest and squeezed his heart tight.

Good grief, Foster. Pull it together.

He was tired. Processing the crime scene, followed by hours of reviewing witness statements and evidence, had worn him down. But the task force was waiting, and as lead investigator, he had a job to do.

Shoving aside his exhaustion, Jonah greeted everyone before attaching two photographs to the whiteboard. "Yesterday, we discovered the bodies of Nolan Carlson and Lisa Valdez. Nolan was 30 years old, blond hair, blue eyes, and worked for a commercial construction firm. He's an outdoor enthusiast who hiked regularly, was part of a rock-climbing group, and traveled frequently to take part in mountain climbing competitions."

He tapped on the second photograph. "Lisa Valdez, 23 years old, brunette hair, brown eyes. A recent college graduate employed as a substitute teacher. Also an outdoor enthusiast, based on her social media posts. She and Nolan got engaged six months ago. They arrived at Piney Woods on Monday afternoon, and according to the initial coroner's report, were killed on Wednesday. That coincides with the cell phone records we've obtained. Lisa and Nolan stopped answering their calls and texts on Wednesday evening around eight o'clock."

"Hold on." Chief Deputy Williams straightened her spine, her brow furrowing. "They were killed *before* Ava and Tyler?"

"Yes. Lisa and Nolan were murdered on Wednesday. Ava and Tyler were killed the next evening on Thursday. The crime scenes bear striking similarities. Both men were shot, both women were sexually assaulted and then manually strangled."

Jonah's voice was flat and clipped as he gave the details, but the crime scene photos taken from the cabin told a horror no one should ever have to face. After Nolan was shot, Lisa attempted to provide first aid, but the killer went after her. She ran. Attempted to escape down the hall, leaving a bloody handprint on the wall.

She fought hard for her life. But it hadn't been enough.

"The state lab compared the bullets removed from the murders. They confirmed the same weapon was used to kill both men. A Ruger SR9 that was recovered from Ava and Tyler's crime scene." Jonah attached a photograph of the weapon to the whiteboard. "Unfortunately, the weapon was in the water when we located it. We couldn't get fingerprints or DNA from it."

"Both women were sexually assaulted." Deputy Nate Martinez looked up from the pad he was taking notes on. His nose was sunburned from being outdoors interviewing campers staying near the cabin. "Was DNA recovered?"

"No. The perpetrator used a condom." Jonah's jaw tightened. "Sexual assault kits were performed on both victims. We recovered trace evidence—fibers, potential skin cells under Lisa's fingernails where she fought back—but nothing definitive yet. The lab is still processing."

Nate nodded. Though he'd initially questioned Jonah's dedication at the first crime scene—protective of his jurisdiction and his sheriff—he'd proven himself to be a team player over the past two days. "There was no sign of forced entry at the cabin, right?"

"Correct. Whoever killed Nolan and Lisa either walked through the unlocked front door or was admitted in by one of them. Nolan's SUV is also missing. A 2018 black Jeep Cherokee. A BOLO has been issued for the vehicle, but it hasn't been found yet."

Jonah moved to a blown-up map of Piney Woods State Park. "Based on the evidence we have so far, the murders happened like this. On Wednesday evening, the perpetrator gained access to Cabin 3. He shot Nolan in the chest before assaulting and strangling Lisa. He leaves the cabin, closing the door behind him. We're not sure how he arrived at the cabin... maybe on foot. Could've been by boat since the cabin is on the lake. Either way, I suspect he stole Nolan's Jeep Cherokee."

Ryker frowned. "Why would the killer steal Nolan's car?"

"He needed a vehicle for the next murder." Laney rose from her chair and joined Jonah at the map. She pointed to Campsite 8. "This is where Ava and Tyler were staying. It's a remote campsite, and unlike Cabin 3, it's not accessible by water because of an overgrowth of reeds. Nor is it easy to walk to. The killer used a suppressor on the Ruger, but it wouldn't have made the gunshots silent. They just reduce the noise. The witness who reported 'fireworks' was driving past on the main road, about two hundred yards away. Even with the suppressor, the shots were loud enough to hear. The killer must've known someone might report them, which meant he needed a fast escape route."

"So he steals his previous victim's vehicle. This way, it won't be traced back to him." Tate whistled. "Whoever this is, he planned out these murders."

"Yes, but he made a few mistakes. Dropping the gun

in the weeds by the lake was one of them. Another was attacking Laney." Jonah's gaze automatically went to the bruises encircling her neck. They'd faded to a sallow yellow but still had the effect of kicking up his protective instincts. "The morning after Ava and Tyler died, someone was lurking outside Laney's cabin. Scout alerted us to his presence. We followed his trail to the lake, where he likely escaped by boat. Later that day, we were followed by a black SUV, similar to Nolan's Jeep Cherokee. Since then, he hasn't made another move. But..."

Ryker's expression darkened as his attention shifted from Jonah to Laney and back again. "You think it's only a matter of time before he does."

"It's been two days." Laney reclaimed her seat at the table. "And the perpetrator hasn't done anything. I'm sure he's figured out that threatening a law enforcement officer would make things worse."

Or he's planning his next move. Jonah had little faith that the murderer would give up easily. The threat that Laney might remember an important detail from the attack was valid. Especially since the killer was probably someone she knew.

Ryker's mouth flattened as he shared a look with Jonah. His wife, Hannah, was a prosecutor. She'd been threatened and nearly killed by a cunning killer determined to protect his identity. Thankfully, the case had been resolved, and she'd made it out unharmed, but the lingering lesson had stuck: Never underestimate the lengths someone would go to avoid prison.

"It stands to reason," Tate said, bringing them back to

the case. "If the perpetrator stole Nolan's car in advance, he had his victims picked out. He knew Ava and Tyler would be at Campsite 8 before they'd even arrived at Piney Woods."

Ryker nodded. "I agree. So, are we looking at a budding serial killer? Or was one couple targeted, and the other killed to muddy the investigation? I think we need to ask Emilia Knox for a consultation. As a profiler, she can help us make sense of what we're looking at here."

Jonah nodded. He'd worked with Emilia before and found her exceptional. She was married to another ranger in Company A, Bennett Knox. "I agree, let's call Emilia in. My gut still says that Ava was the primary target." He winced internally, thinking of the crime scene photos. "The killer spent more time with her. According to the coroner, she was alive longer during the assault. The strangulation was slower, more deliberate. With Lisa, it was faster—almost clinical."

There had been a coldness to the scene in Cabin 3, to Nolan and Lisa's murders. As if the perpetrator had used them for practice. "I think whoever did this murdered the first couple to muddy the waters of the investigation, to make us think everything was random."

"If that's true," Tate added. "Then Garrett is the most likely suspect. He harassed Ava and admitted that he was romantically interested in her. He also lied about his alibi. He couldn't have been with Lisa and Nolan on Thursday night since they were already dead."

"I've been mulling that over and can't make heads or tails of it." Chief Deputy Williams beat her pen against her pad. "If Garrett killed these couples, why would he offer Nolan and Lisa as his alibi? He knew we'd go to their cabin to question them."

"Maybe that was the intent. He wanted us to find the bodies."

The room was silent as the weight of that sank into everyone.

"I attempted to question Garrett after discovering Nolan and Lisa's bodies. Unfortunately, he's invoked his right to counsel, and his attorney won't allow him to answer questions. I applied for a search warrant for his home and business. We executed it this morning."

"And?" Ryker leaned forward.

"Nothing. No stolen Jeep Cherokee. No suppressor. No bloody clothing. His computers and phone are with forensics, but his lawyer is already filing motions to suppress anything they find, arguing the harassment allegations don't justify searching his digital life." Jonah's frustration bled through. "We've caught him lying about his alibi, but his lawyer claims he just mixed up the days, and without physical evidence tying him to the crime scenes, we can't arrest him."

Tate squinted at the board. "Garrett's an outdoorsman. Does he have a boat?"

"If so, it's not registered or moored at any of the local marinas."

"A small dinghy or kayak is easy to keep in a cove somewhere on the lake," Laney added. "It's not legal, but people do it all the time. Someone like Garrett, who has intimate knowledge of the lake and hiking trails, wouldn't have any trouble finding an out of way place to store a small boat."

"What about phone records?" Ryker asked. "Garrett's phone could've pinged off a local tower, which would help place him near Cabin 3 or Campsite 8 at the time of the attacks."

"I've requested it, but the phone company said it'll take 48 hours. We should have it by Wednesday morning. But I'm not hopeful it'll help. Someone smart enough to steal a previous victim's vehicle and use it to commit a second murder has the brains to leave his cell phone at home." Jonah placed his hands on the back of a chair and nodded at Deputy Martinez. "The sheriff's department will monitor Garrett's home and business."

"We need to tread carefully here. Garrett's lawyered up, and his defense attorney will argue we had tunnel-vision when it came to his client and ignored other viable suspects. We need to question and eliminate anyone else who could've committed these crimes." Ryker turned toward Laney. "What do your records show about the time Ava volunteered here at the park?"

"She was sporadic, pitching in mostly during big events. The last time she volunteered was during the Spring Jamboree. It's a week-long event taking place during spring break with activities ranging from trail hikes to craft making." Laney referred to her notes. "Ava volunteered for a couple of days and worked at the wildlife center. Ranger Zoe Papadopoulos oversaw the program, assisted by Eddie Sorenson."

"Eddie Sorenson?" Jonah straightened. "He didn't

mention working with Ava when we interviewed him the day after the murders."

"He may not remember her. There were 50 volunteers coming and going in the wildlife program. Ranger Papadopoulos didn't remember her. Neither did I." Laney and Jonah had interviewed all the rangers on her staff. No one recalled Ava. "Honestly, people run together unless they volunteer with us year after year. As I said, Ava was sporadic."

"Hold on." Tate was ruffling through papers. "I'm still working my way through the background checks of staff members, but I found something on Eddie Sorenson that I wanted to mention during the meeting."

He found the paper he was looking for and offered it to Jonah. "Eddie's background check came back clear, but his ex-wife filed a restraining order on him about a year ago while they were going through their divorce. She claimed he slapped her across the face during an argument. He also showed up at her home at all hours of the day and night."

Laney looked dumbfounded. Her mouth dropped open, and she struggled for a moment before saying, "I've never seen a hint of anger from Eddie, even during stressful situations. What happened to the restraining order?"

"It expired, and the ex-wife never renewed it."

Chief Deputy Williams leaned back in her chair. "I know Eddie Sorenson. My sister is married to his cousin. Eddie's divorce was contentious, and his ex-wife unsupportive and not well liked in the family. I have to side with Laney here. Eddie's not the violent type."

Jonah respected her opinion. And Laney's. But cunning people could hide their dark side. He'd seen it too many times in his career. "Still, we need to question Eddie again. I'll handle that."

Laney's jaw tightened. "I'm going with you."

THIRTEEN

Dark clouds hid the sun, heavy with the promise of rain. Laney kept pace with Jonah as he headed for the boathouse. She was reeling from the news that Eddie's ex-wife had taken out a restraining order against him. It seemed hard to believe, so when she spotted her deputy ranger, Andy, speaking with Zoe near a park bench, she touched Jonah's arm.

"Wait, before we talk to Eddie, I want to speak to Zoe again about Ava's volunteer work this spring. And I'd like to know if Andy had any knowledge of the restraining order."

Every piece of information they gathered would help suss out whether Eddie was telling the truth. She preferred to have as many answers to her questions as possible before interviewing a person of interest.

Jonah nodded, and then he fell into step beside her as she moved to join them. Zoe spotted them first, her lips curving up into a welcoming smile. Her ranger uniform was dusty, as if she'd been hiking the trails, and in one hand, she held a canteen of water. "Hey, boss, good timing. We were just talking about you."

"How come?" Laney asked, coming to a stop in the grass. She expected to feel Scout beside her but then remembered she'd left the dog in the conference room with Ryker and Tate. Scout was getting up there in years and needed more rest.

"We need to complete the agenda for the TDPW site inspection on Tuesday morning," Zoe said.

Laney's stomach dropped. She'd completely forgotten. The TDPW had scheduled this months ago, and as acting superintendent, it was imperative that she be in attendance. She'd been planning for weeks to ask them to increase the budget for projects and repairs that needed to be made. "Tuesday morning."

"Ten o'clock," Andy supplied, adjusting his ranger hat against the threatening weather. The lines in his weathered face were deeper, and he looked as exhausted as Laney felt. "They want a full tour of the facilities, then a working lunch meeting to discuss budget priorities and operational challenges."

He gave her a pointed look. One that needed no interpretation. Screwing up this meeting would sink any chance she would have of being superintendent. If she wanted the job.

With everything going on, Laney hadn't even had time to think about it.

Regardless, she couldn't blow this meeting off. For the park's sake, if not her own. Convincing TDPW to increase their annual budget would go a long way toward funding necessary upgrades. "Let's set a time to go over the final details." She checked her schedule on her phone. "Two o'clock tomorrow work for everyone?"

Both Andy and Zoe agreed. Laney made a note in her calendar. With that matter handled, she moved on. "Zoe, it's come to my attention that Ava Morrison volunteered here. In fact, she worked our Spring Jamboree last year, in the wildlife center."

Zoe gasped, bringing a hand to her mouth. "That's why she looked so familiar to me. I kept staring at her picture, thinking I recognized her from somewhere, but dismissed the notion as a figment of my imagination." She lowered her hand, her expression troubled.

"Do you remember working with her?" Jonah asked.

"No. We had so many volunteers that week..." Zoe pulled out her phone. "Wait, let me check something. I email out the volunteer schedule at the beginning of each event." She tapped on her screen, scrolling through old messages. "Here—Spring Jamboree, March 18th. I sent the assignments to all the volunteers and staff supervisors."

She squinted at her phone, reading. "Ava Morrison... yes, she's on here. Assigned to the wildlife center for three days, Wednesday through Friday of that week. Eddie Sorenson was her direct supervisor." Zoe looked up. "She was one of his volunteers. He would've worked with her directly. Maybe he remembers more about her."

"We'll check with him," Laney said. "Speaking of Eddie, I know there were some challenges with him during the Spring Jamboree. Do you recall if he had any troublesome interactions with volunteers or issues with anyone on staff?"

"No, Eddie gets along great with everyone. My biggest issues with him were work related. Showing up late, slacking on projects, sloppiness. Every time I called him out on it, he always apologized. I think he was just going through a rough time back then. His dad had just died, and Eddie took it hard. Plus, he was in the midst of a troublesome divorce. His wife had never gotten along with his family, and Eddie knew they had real problems in the marriage, but he was brokenhearted about the separation." A blush crept across her cheeks. "I covered for him more than I should have, but I felt bad about what he was going through."

"I understand." Laney would never fault one of her subordinates for having a kind heart. And Zoe's description of Eddie was similar to her own. A small measure of comfort. "Thanks for your help. I'll see you tomorrow."

Zoe gave a small wave and then strolled away.

Laney waited until she was out of earshot before turning to face her chief ranger. "Were you aware that Eddie's wife took out a restraining order against him?"

Andy blinked in shock, his mouth falling open. It was rare to catch the older man by surprise. "Absolutely not." His gaze skipped to Jonah before landing back on Laney. "You... you think *Eddie* committed these murders?"

No, she didn't, but that wasn't the point. "He's keeping secrets. Eddie didn't mention working with Ava during the Spring Jamboree, nor did he tell us about the restraining order. How I feel about Eddie is irrelevant. We have to follow the evidence where it leads us."

Andy mulled that over for a minute and dipped his chin. "You're right. I just... I find it hard to believe he had anything to do with this."

"Do me a favor. Reach out to the people on Zoe's schedule who were in the wildlife center at the same time as Ava. See if any of them remember her or Eddie. Frame it as routine follow-up for the investigation. Don't mention that Eddie's a person of interest."

He nodded sharply. "You got it."

Laney started to turn away and then stopped. "Oh, and Andy, please be discreet. We don't know with any certainty that Eddie is involved. I don't want to damage his reputation, especially if there's an innocent explanation."

"Understood."

His expression was troubled. Laney could tell Andy didn't like the idea of one of their own being responsible for these heinous crimes any more than she did. She couldn't walk away without giving him some measure of comfort. "Try not to worry. We'll figure this out."

He nodded and then ambled toward the visitor center, his gait slower than she remembered. He suddenly looked... old. Andy had worked for the park service for nearly thirty years. He'd made it clear he didn't want the superintendent job. None of the other rangers on staff had enough experience to take on the challenge. Which meant that if Laney didn't take the job, they would have to bring in someone from outside Piney

Woods. Someone who may not agree with the programs they created or their renovation plans.

Someone who might not care about the employees the way she did...

Guilt swamped her. How could she walk away from this promotion? The thought was followed immediately by a sense of panic and dread. Taking the job would mean staying here permanently... something she'd never planned on or wanted.

"You okay?" Jonah's question jolted Laney out of her thoughts. "You went a million miles away."

She shook her head. "Sorry. Just thinking. Let's get this over with." Laney crossed the grass toward the boathouse. Movement near the dock caught her eye. A man was fishing in the restricted section near the rental area. She altered course, Jonah following.

The fisherman wore scuffed tennis shoes, a sweat-stained gray T-shirt, and a faded red ball cap pulled low over his eyes. His fishing pole looked worse for wear, with duct tape holding the reel assembly together. A scraggly beard covered the lower half of his face, and he had the weathered, sun-damaged skin of someone who spent most of their time outdoors. He didn't notice their approach, focused on his line.

"Excuse me, sir," Laney called out.

The man's head jerked up, his muddy brown eyes widening beneath the brim of his cap. Up close, she could see the nervous tension in his posture. His gaze shot from her to Jonah. His fishing pole trembled.

"You can't fish here. This area is reserved for boat

rentals and swimming. There's designated fishing spots marked on the map at the visitor center, or you can fish from the north shore."

"Oh. Yeah. Sorry." His words were hurried, and he immediately started reeling in his line, the movements jerky. "Didn't know. I'll move."

"No problem. Just check the park map next time. And make sure you have a valid fishing license. It's required."

He bobbed his head without making eye contact, already gathering his tackle box. Within seconds, he'd packed up and was heading toward the tree line at a brisk walk.

Laney watched him go for a moment before turning back toward the boathouse.

"He was nervous," Jonah observed.

"Probably afraid I was going to cite him. Sometimes, people who are food insecure or homeless come here to fish, and don't have a permit. I don't like to write them up unless they continually violate the rules."

They reached the boathouse. Through the open bay doors, Laney could see the Sunday afternoon rush in full swing. A family of four clustered around the rental counter, the parents debating between kayaks and canoes while their kids bounced with impatience. Two college-aged guys were hauling life jackets from the storage racks, and a young couple stood near the dock studying a laminated map of the lake's best fishing spots.

Eddie stood behind the counter processing paperwork, while Marcus Garcia—one of their weekend staff—

helped the family select paddle sizes. The hum of activity and chatter filled the space, punctuated by the slap of water against the dock pilings.

Not ideal for a sensitive interview.

Laney caught Eddie's eye and gestured toward the door. He said something to Marcus, and then made his way over, wiping his hands on a towel tucked into his belt. Laney led him out into the gray afternoon and around the corner to a quiet picnic bench out of the sight of others. "Have a seat, Eddie."

"Is there a problem, ma'am?" His Adam's apple bobbed, but he did as she requested, folding his long legs underneath the table. The wind ruffled his hair, revealing some gray at the temples. Dark circles ringed his eyes. It didn't look like Eddie was getting much sleep.

"We need to ask you a few more questions about Ava." She kept her voice neutral, but her gaze was locked on the other man. Jonah had planted himself a short distance away, leaning casually on a nearby tree. Close enough to hear the conversation, but far enough away so as not to be intimidating. A calculated move, Laney was sure. They needed Eddie to feel comfortable enough to talk. "Why didn't you mention Ava was a volunteer at Piney Woods?"

Eddie blinked. "She was?"

Playing stupid? Or genuinely confused? Laney couldn't tell. "She worked with you during the Spring Jamboree in the wildlife center. You were her direct supervisor."

His cheeks heated, and his gaze slid away from hers.

"Last spring was a hectic time. I... I had no idea... I didn't remember her. We had a lot of volunteers for the Jamboree and..." He pulled at the collar of his shirt as his explanation drifted off. "Is that important?"

"Right now, everything is important."

His leg jittered underneath the table. "Oh, okay."

Laney let the silence drift. A tactic that usually got people talking. Eddie, however, didn't rush to fill the quiet. His attention was locked on a leaf resting on the table, and his leg never stopped moving. Laney switched directions. "I remember the Spring Jamboree was a rough time for you. Your dad had recently passed, and you were going through a divorce."

Eddie nodded but didn't add any additional details.

"Why didn't you tell me that your ex-wife took out a restraining order against you?"

He jolted, his gaze shooting straight to her. Something akin to panic crept across his face, deepening the lines around his mouth. "It's not what you think, ma'am." The words came fast, nearly running together in his rush to get them out.

Laney gave him a reassuring look. "Okay. Tell me then."

Eddie licked his lips. "Our divorce was contentious. My ex-wife has a temper, and she didn't like that I got to stay in our family home. The house had been a gift from my dad. It was mine outright, and not part of the marital property. She..." He wiped a bead of sweat from his forehead. "She would drive over to the house and break things. A planter hanging from the porch, the front window. Then she started leaving nasty stuff on my doorstep. It was... it was bad."

His fingers began tapping against the table. "I should have let it go, but I was grieving and not in the best headspace. I drove to her house and confronted her. We got into a heated argument, and as I turned to leave, she grabbed my arm. I tried to free myself and accidentally smacked her in the face." He stilled, his jaw tightening. "The next day, she filed a restraining order against me. I realized what a foolish idiot I'd been. I stayed clear of her after that."

His eyes lifted to hers, his expression nearly pleading. "I should have told you. I know. But I didn't want to lose my job. I love it here..." He drew in a shaky breath. "I'm sorry."

Laney let that sit for a moment. His apology and his explanation seemed sincere, but she couldn't ignore the fact that he also seemed nervous. Eddie didn't have a solid alibi for Ava and Tyler's murder. He claimed to have gone home and watched a game. She waited a beat and asked, "I assume you've heard about the murders in Cabin 3."

He nodded, his gaze once again skittering away from hers.

"Did you know Nolan Carlson or Lisa Valdez?"

"No."

That could be true. She'd checked the boat rentals, and neither Nolan nor Lisa had come up. "Where were you on Wednesday night between the hours of seven and midnight?"

"Uhhh, Wednesday?" He seemed to search for the answer in the leaf on the table. "I'm sure I was at home. I'm there most nights."

"Can anyone vouch for that? Did you make a phone call? Or see anyone?"

His jaw tightened, and he shook his head. He still wouldn't look at her. And his leg was jittering again. Laney considered pressing, but she didn't see the point. It would be better to hear from other volunteers who had worked with Ava and Eddie first. Then she might have something more concrete to challenge him on. "Okay, Eddie. Thanks for talking with us. You can go back to work now."

His head jerked up. "You... you aren't going to fire me?"

"No. We'll need to deal with your lack of transparency about the restraining order, but I want to think about it and consult with Andy before any final decisions are made."

If Eddie's story turned out to be true, she didn't want to penalize him for a mistake. Romantic relationships could be messy, and she could understand that Eddie might've been embarrassed and upset about the restraining order. He still should have told them, but that error in judgment didn't erase his years of park service.

Eddie popped up. "Thank you, ma'am." With a nod in Jonah's direction, he headed for the boathouse. His stride was rapid, as if he couldn't get away fast enough.

Jonah sighed before joining Laney at the picnic table. He sat shoulder to shoulder with her in silence for a while, and the warmth of his arm pressed against hers was distracting. She was all too aware of his breathing, the subtle scent of peppermint from his frequent use of breath mints, the way his hand rested just inches from hers on the weathered table. Finally, he said, "You know he's lying, don't you?"

"About which part?"

"The details about the argument with his wife. Definitely about where he was on Wednesday night."

Disappointment settled inside her like a stone. "I know."

Eddie was hiding something. That was very clear.

But was it murder?

Her cell phone beeped with an incoming text message. Laney pulled it from her pocket and glanced at the screen, a smile tugging at her lips. "It's Breanna. She's inviting us to have dinner with her. Pizza." The phone beeped again, and this time, Laney laughed. "She's also asking us to bring the pizza."

"Tell her yes."

She turned and eyed Jonah. "You sure? You've been running on fumes, and I know socializing takes a lot out of you." They'd attended church this morning, and Jonah had been pretty quiet throughout the service. He talked less and less the more tired he became. "I don't mind skipping it. We can have dinner with them another night."

"A break from the case would do us both good." His expression was warm, and when the breeze lifted a stray strand of her hair across her cheek, Jonah reached out to push it back. The move was unexpected. Not part of their usual friendship dance. Laney's pulse jumped, and she froze at the sudden contact. His fingers left a trail of heat in their wake. Butterflies ignited.

Jonah seemed to take his time, moving slowly. Deliberately. His thumb brushed along the sensitive curve of her ear, and her breath hitched. "Arrange dinner with your sister, Laney. I'd be happy to go with you."

FOURTEEN

Jonah wiped his hands on a dish towel before hanging it on a hook next to the sink. "More hot cocoa, Papa Earl?"

"No, thank you, son." His lips quirked, one side drooping because of the stroke he'd had over the summer. "Two cups is all I can handle. Gotta watch my waistline."

The older man cracked up, and Jonah chuckled along with him. Earl Sullivan had always been a jokester. He was also rail thin. Too thin after the stroke and could stand to put on a few pounds. At eighty-four, his hair was more gray than black. Lines etched in his ochre face spoke of happiness and hard work. He'd spent decades working in a factory, raising kids, and taking care of his wife. Since the passing of his beloved Mary three years ago, he'd been lost. Moving in with Marcus, Breanna, and baby Asher returned some of the sparkle to his eyes.

"How did your last doctor's appointment go?" Jonah asked, leaning against the counter.

Papa Earl beamed. "Doctor says I'm a champion." He

thumped his chest with a shaky fist. "The most progress of any patient he's seen this month. He wants me to continue on with my physical therapy though. Said something about gaining more function or something or other."

"That's great news. You'll be running laps around us in no time."

"You can bet on it." His expression grew serious. "I heard about the murders at the park. Nasty business. How you holding up, son? Working a case like that must take a toll on a man's spirit. Not to mention having Laney mixed up in all this. That makes it personal."

"I'll feel a lot better once the perpetrator is behind bars."

Papa Earl studied him for a long moment. His dark eyes were pensive. "One thing about my stroke... I've stopped beating around the bush. How long are you gonna keep pretending you aren't in love with that girl?"

Jonah stiffened and then automatically glanced over his shoulder. Through a small cutout, he could see into the living room. Music was playing. Laney sat on the floor gently rocking Asher, his sweet face half hidden by a pacifier. Next to her, Breanna held a handful of paint colors. The two of them were deep in discussion about the right color for the living room. Scout snoozed nearby.

He swung his gaze back to Papa Earl. "Laney and I are just friends. That's all we've been for a long time."

"Doesn't mean you don't want more."

"She doesn't."

"You sure about that? People change. They grow."

The old man's comments brought to mind the way

Laney kept sneaking glances at him when she thought he wasn't looking. Jonah hadn't noticed until their awkward interaction in the car, when he thought something was on his face. Laney's blush had confused him. But since then, he'd picked up on small tells that ignited a bit of hope that was unwise to feed. Testing the waters today by brushing the strand of hair away from her face... hearing her breath hitch and seeing the way her eyes darkened... it was playing with fire.

"Laney's not one to invest in romantic relationships." Jonah gripped the counter. He'd already been a casualty of her inability to commit. "It's not worth losing my best friend over."

The older man grunted. Then he started to stand. Jonah deftly stepped forward and moved his walker closer. Papa Earl thanked him, gripping the metal frame tightly with his right hand. The other drooped at his side. "I'll tell you what, son, time doesn't wait for any man. And the worst thing you can have is regret. Don't let your fear be the reason you hold back."

Jonah's brow crinkled, even as his heart skipped a beat. "Did... did Laney say something to you?"

"Heavens no. I know better than to stick my nose in women's business. My dear Mary taught me that, may she rest in peace." Papa Earl pegged him with a look. "But I've earned the right to meddle a little in a man's business. Sometimes, you boys need an old codger to point out what's plain as day."

He laughed. The advice wasn't something he'd take,

but he appreciated how much Papa Earl cared. "Guess I should thank you for the kick in the pants?"

Papa Earl snorted, but his mouth twitched with amusement. "You won't though. I was the same at your age. A know-it-all." He shuffled toward the living room. "Time to take these old bones to bed. Goodnight."

"Night." He shook his head, bemused by Papa Earl. He collected the last of the dessert plates and mugs from the table. The sound of Earl saying good night to Breanna and Laney filtered through the cut-out.

While loading the dishwasher and wiping the counter, Jonah replayed the conversation with Papa Earl. Clearly, he wasn't doing a good job of keeping his emotions in check. The last thing he wanted was for Laney to get a whiff of them. It would send her running so far so fast, their friendship might never recover. At the very least, it would make things incredibly awkward.

His focus needed to be on catching a killer.

Mind made up, he once again wiped his hands on the dish towel and hung it up before going into the living room. Laney looked up as he entered, her soft smile warming him straight through. She was still holding Asher. The infant was nestled against her chest, wrapped in a blanket with teddy bears marching across. His dark hair was so similar to hers, Jonah's mind momentarily imagined she was holding her own child.

Like an ice pick, the thought shattered his resolve. Would Laney get married one day? Have kids of her own? Surely, she wouldn't run away from romantic relationships forever. Her last relationship with Mike had lasted longer than the others. At some point, the right guy would come along.

The idea of her married to someone else... it hit hard.

"Earth to Jonah." Laney snapped her fingers, a smile tugging at her lips, but there was concern in her eyes. "Are you sleeping with your eyes open?"

He blinked, belatedly realizing Breanna was at his side holding out two paint colors. Jonah scrubbed a hand over his face. "Sorry, I think I am. What were you asking me, Bre?"

"Which one?" She held out two shades of nearly identical gray swatches of paint. Petite and dark-haired, Breanna was an interesting mixture of practical and whimsical. She wore sensible jeans and sneakers but had paired them with a flowing floral blouse and delicate silver earrings that caught the light when she moved.

"Uhhh, those colors look the same to me." Jonah shot a questioning glance toward Laney who pressed her lips together to keep from laughing and shook her head. She tried to use the couch to get up off the floor, but tilted backward. Without hesitation, Jonah caught her.

For a moment, they were frozen like that—him leaning over her, his hands holding on to her waist, baby Asher safely secure between them. Laney's gorgeous brown eyes went wide as they met his. Her lips parted, and he felt her sharp intake of breath. Something flickered across her face—surprise, maybe confusion—before she quickly looked away and murmured, "thanks."

Jonah released her and took a giant step back. What

was *wrong* with him? Exhaustion. That had to be it. He rubbed a hand over his face. "I'm fading fast."

"We should head back. I'm tired too." Laney handed Asher to her sister. "Go with Mindful Gray, Bre. It has a touch of blue that will make the yellow in your wood floor pop."

They said their goodbyes and stepped into the night. It smelled like rain. The weather reports predicted thunderstorms over the next couple of days. Jonah sank into the passenger seat, thankful he wasn't driving. He glanced worriedly in Laney's direction. Piney Woods was only fifteen minutes away, but she had to be nearly as tired as he was. "Sure you can get us home safely?"

"Yeah, I'm fine. Don't worry." She backed out of the drive and steered them toward Piney Woods. "It was nice to take a couple of hours off from the case. Thanks for agreeing to have dinner."

"It's not a hardship. Breanna and Papa Earl are like family, although I was sorry Marcus couldn't join us."

Marcus worked nights as a nurse and had been on duty. Jonah leaned his head against the seat rest. Behind him, Scout shifted in her crate before settling down with a sigh. "Did you tell Breanna about your potential promotion? The superintendent position?"

"No. I'm not sure I'm going to take it, and I don't want to get her hopes up that I'll settle in town permanently." A troubled look crossed her face. "It'll be hard to leave if I decide to turn it down though. Asher is so cute, and it's been nice being close enough to see them all the time."

Those sounded like two good reasons to stay, but Jonah didn't want to add to her worries. There was plenty of time to discuss the promotion after the murder case was solved. "Bre seems really happy to me. Content. Motherhood suits her."

"It does. And Marcus is a great dad."

There was a hint of sadness in her voice he couldn't quite place. Jonah wondered if she was thinking about her own father. Laney rarely talked about him, or the pain that followed when he left. In his opinion, Antonio Torres was a world class fool to trade his wife and daughters for a mistress.

They arrived at Laney's cabin. The moon was hidden behind clouds, the only illumination from the light on the front porch. Jonah scanned the surrounding area before escorting her to the door. Laney was pensive. Unusually so. He had the notion that she wasn't ready for him to leave yet. "Any chance you could make me a cup of that sleepy tea? I had coffee at Bre's and now I feel wired."

She flashed him a bright smile. "Of course."

He halted her movement before she stepped inside the house. "Let me sweep it. Just to be sure." Jonah crossed over the threshold, hand on his holstered weapon, and paused. He didn't sense anyone inside the house. Still, he went through the small cabin, checking closets and under the bed anyway. The space was neat and simply decorated.

Two photos were on her nightstand. One of Laney with her mother and Breanna. The other was of him and Laney, taken during a trip to the Grand Canyon the summer after he'd been injured in the line of duty. Both of them wore sunglasses and wide smiles. He remembered being thrilled that he'd made it up the mountain. The doctors had worried the compound fractures in his arm and leg, earned while tackling a perpetrator, would leave him with permanent mobility issues. He'd feared his career in law enforcement was over. But Laney hadn't let him give up. She dropped everything to take care of him, camping out in his living room and refusing to leave until he was—quite literally—back on his feet.

Setting the photo back on her nightstand, he went into the living room. Laney was talking to Scout in the kitchen. Jonah collapsed on the couch and turned on a basketball game but left the sound off. He watched without really paying attention.

Moments later, Scout jumped on the couch next to him. She licked his face. He laughingly pushed her away. "Love you too, Scout." He stroked her fur, and she settled next to him just as Laney appeared, carrying two cups of tea. She handed one to him.

"For someone who doesn't play sports, you sure watch a lot of them." She tucked her feet up under her as she claimed the other corner of the couch.

"Habit. There was always a game on in my house growing up." He blew on the tea before taking a sip. It was light and floral smelling. Jonah resisted the urge to wrinkle his nose. He wasn't a fan of her sleepy tea and had only used the suggestion as an excuse to stay until she was at ease.

"How is your family? You haven't said much about them."

"Same old, same old. Cathy's team won state this year, so the university signed her for another million years, and Samuel saved about a thousand lives with his magical surgeon hands. The July fourth family barbecue was a torrent of accomplishments." He offered her a rueful smile to take the sting out of his words. Jonah was proud of his family. He was. But being around them was a constant reminder of how different he was from the rest of them. "I thought about sharing some of my murder cases, but it's not polite conversation to have over brisket and coleslaw."

She chuckled. "I suppose that's true." Laney reached across and took his hand. "But I wouldn't sell yourself short either. What you do is important, Jonah. It's not flashy and it won't make you rich, but at the end of the day, none of that really matters. What counts is the kind of person you are."

"My family has never seen it that way."

"I know. But it's their loss. And I pray that one day, God will change their hearts. You deserve to be seen for the amazing person you are by the people you love the most."

Jonah's throat tightened at her words. He was secure in his career, but in his personal life... he felt adrift. Confused. Never quite good enough. He looked down at their joined hands, the way Laney's delicate fingers were so feminine next to his thicker ones. The longing was nearly painful. But fear kept the truth buried, where it was safe. He'd been honest when he'd told Papa Earl that whatever his feelings for Laney, it wasn't worth risking their friendship over.

It was late, and Jonah knew he should leave, but now he was the one who wasn't ready. "Watch the game with me?"

She gave a soft smile. "Sure."

He leaned back against the couch, letting the weight of his exhaustion settle over him. And then suddenly, he jerked awake. His eyes struggled to adjust to the dark, and his mind didn't know where he was. Jonah blinked. Laney's cabin. He must've fallen asleep on the couch. A blanket covered his body, and the television was off. What time was it? A quick check of his watch confirmed it was almost five in the morning.

That's when he heard it. The noise that must've woken him from a dead sleep.

Scout.

She stood in the kitchen doorway. Her body was tense in the dim glow from the nightlight in the small hall, gaze focused on the back door. She bared her teeth.

Her growl was low and threatening.

FIFTEEN

In a second, Jonah was on his feet. His hand flew to the weapon at his side, but the holster was empty. Panic tightened his chest until he spotted his gun sitting, magazine out, on the coffee table. Laney must've removed it while he was sleeping for safety. He scooped up the Glock and shoved the magazine home while taking three long strides across the small living room to Scout's side.

She growled again, her hackles raised, entire body tense.

"What is it, girl?" He peered out the small window over the sink into the yard. The predawn light cast everything in a ghostly blue-gray hue. A light drizzle pattered against the roof. The pine trees swayed in the breeze, their needled branches creating shifting patterns against the gradually brightening sky. Between their trunks, darkness pooled.

Jonah edged past Scout and shifted next to the door for a better view of the yard. The lake was a dark blot, the water rippling with the rain. He scanned the tree line. Nothing shifted. Scout joined him, sitting on her haunches. Her dark brown eyes looked up at him questioningly.

He felt slightly stupid, but that didn't stop him from whispering. "I don't see anything. If you are causing all of this ruckus because of a raccoon, we're gonna have words."

Her brows dropped into a furrow, and Jonah shook his head. "Okay, okay. I believe you." He scanned the yard again, focusing on the trees in the distance. Nothing stirred. Had the trespasser fled? Likely, since Scout had relaxed. He shifted to the window over the sink again. A flash of something caught his eye. Not in the yard. No, much closer.

Hanging from the corner of the porch was a small dead animal.

Anger, fast and sharp, burst through him. He moved back to the door and twisted the knob. Scout rose. He gently pushed her out of the way, blocking her ability to go outside. Jonah didn't want the dog to get hurt on the off-chance the perpetrator was still lurking nearby.

Moist air coated his skin as he stepped outside, closing the door behind him. Cautiously, keeping to the shadow of the cabin, he edged along the porch. His gaze roamed the area beyond the yard. A brave squirrel bounced down an oak tree and jumped toward a pine. The rain picked up speed. Its steady drumbeat was in rapid tune with his heart. He approached the dead animal.

A rabbit. Likely a wild one, judging from its dark brown fur. Its head was twisted at an unnatural angle, its tongue stuck out. A strand of barbed wire wrapped around its neck. The other end was attached to a hook meant for plants on the roof of the porch. It took Jonah a moment to realize it wasn't just rain darkening the poor animal's fur. It was blood.

The wind gusted. The rabbit turned in slow motion as if touched by an invisible hand, revealing a note attached to its side. Jonah's muscles tensed. He leaned in to read the typewritten message.

Be afraid, little bunny. Be very afraid.

A cold chill ran down his spine, and Jonah's fingers tightened on his Glock. Whoever was behind this wasn't simply trying to silence Laney, he wanted to terrorize her. The realization hit him like a physical blow. What kind of sick game was this? What did the killer want? It didn't make sense.

Jonah went down the porch steps and into the yard. Rain damped his hair and his shirt, chilling his skin. Depressions in the grass indicated the path the perpetrator had taken.

A gasp came from behind him. He whirled to find Laney standing on the porch in her pajamas and a pair of ratty tennis shoes. In one hand, she held her service weapon. Her attention was locked on the rabbit. In a blink, her shock disappeared, replaced by a fiery rage he didn't see very often.

The truth crystallized in an instant. The reason the killer had left the rabbit on the porch.

Desperation took hold, even as he took one step toward Laney, and barked, "Get back inside—"

Gunshots erupted.

Glass shattered as the bullets slammed into the window next to Laney. She dropped to the floor. Jonah hit the ground, rolling behind the corner of the house for cover, losing sight of Laney in the process. Bullets slammed into the wooden porch in rapid succession. Scout erupted into frantic barks and then fell silent. His heart dropped. My God, had the dog been hit? Had Laney?

Jonah rose to a crouched position, weapon at the ready. His heart thundered. Concern for Laney threatened to unmoor him, but he forced it away. The gunman was hidden in a copse of trees. He gauged the shooter's position and took aim, firing off a couple of rounds.

The bullets flying their way ceased.

He waited with bated breath. A heartbeat later, the sound of someone crashing through the woods shattered the silence. Scout barked, and then Laney's voice cut through the morning air from somewhere near the front of the cabin.

"Jonah! You okay?"

"I'm fine!" he called back. "Stay down!"

But instead of staying put, he heard her tennis shoes hit the porch. He popped his head around the corner of the house in time to see her vault over the railing and take off across the grass in pursuit of the shooter. With an uncharacteristic curse, Jonah bolted after her. "Stop! Laney!"

She paid him no heed. Wet branches smacked him in the face as he tried to catch up to her. His cowboy boots slid on the soft ground, made slippery by last night's thunderstorm. He didn't know these woods. Not like Laney, and clearly not like the killer either. Both of them had disappeared into the trees. Panic pulsed through him, fast and hot, mingling with a fear that threatened to send him straight over the edge.

Jonah pressed forward. The snap of breaking branches ahead told him which direction she'd gone. He followed the sound of her pursuit—shoes on wet leaves, the rustle of disturbed undergrowth. When the sounds faded, his heart hammered harder.

He slid to a stop under an oak. Rain beat down on his head and shoulders. He turned in a circle, desperately searching for a clue that would put him back on Laney's path, praying that the next noise he heard wouldn't be gunshots.

Please, God. Please. Help me.

The rumble of an engine broke through the silence. Without hesitation, Jonah bolted in the direction it came from. Gunshots sent his pulse into overdrive. He burst out of the trees and onto the shore of the lake. Laney stood a short distance away behind a tree, gun raised. A small motorboat raced across the water. Whoever was driving was crouched down, nothing more than a black blob against a gray sky.

Laney spun in Jonah's direction. When she saw him, she lowered her weapon. "He got away."

He got away. He got away.

The words whipped through his head on repeat like a hurricane, even as his gaze swept over her slender form. Rain had soaked her hair, leaving the black strands clumped and causing rivulets to chase down her face into the collar of her pajama top. Her ratty tennis shoes were coated with damp grass. But there was no blood. She was whole. Unharmed. Alive.

And a rage unlike anything Jonah had ever experienced before coursed through him. It was nearly blinding. The worry and panic and desperation all tangled together like three bolts of lightning hitting the same metal rod.

"How could you be so reckless?" He shouted the words. Yelling wasn't something he did. Ever. But at this moment, Jonah couldn't control his emotions. He stalked toward her. "Don't ever do that again. Do you hear me?" His hand shot out and grabbed her arm, pulling her closer. "You could've been killed!"

Shock widened her eyes. "Jonah—"

"No!" He couldn't hear her explanation. Didn't want it. He was practically vibrating with the force of his feelings. A tidal wave of emotion that couldn't be held back. "You can't take risks like that. Don't you understand that there are people who depend on you? People who love you."

In that moment, he got it. What Papa Earl had been trying to say.

Time waits for no man.

And Jonah... he'd wasted so much time. That's what this was all about. The bruises on Laney's neck were still visible, proof of how close she'd come to losing her life. And still, he hadn't understood. But now, standing in the shelter of a pine tree, the rain beating down on both of them... he got it. One bullet could have ended any chance he'd had.

Laney's hand landed on his chest, right over his pounding heart. Something flickered in her eyes as she looked up at him. Not fear or confusion, but recognition. As if she were seeing him clearly for the first time, understanding what he was really saying.

And then her gaze dropped to his mouth.

He didn't think. Didn't pause. His feelings were too raw, too exposed, to stay hidden.

And so, driven by years of pent-up emotion, Jonah bent his head and kissed her.

SIXTEEN

His mouth was warm.

Surprise froze Laney in place the moment Jonah kissed her, but in the next heartbeat, it was consumed by a fierce hunger she'd never experienced before. Need coiled in her belly. Her fingers curled into his shirt, pulling him closer, and she kissed him back with a desperation that matched his own. The world narrowed to the taste of rain on his lips and the solid warmth of his body pressed against hers. The intensity of it tilted her world on its axis. It also set off alarm bells.

With a sharp inhale, she broke the kiss. Chest heaving, fear slicing through her, Laney shoved away from Jonah, forcing him to break his hold. Oh, God, what had she done? What had *they* done? Numbness spread through her limbs as a rising sense of panic narrowed her vision.

"Laney." Jonah's voice was husky and more than a bit shaky.

She couldn't. Couldn't look him in the eye. Couldn't talk about this.

"We..." Her brain scrambled to find a safe topic to cling to. "We should call this in. The sheriff's department might be able to get someone out on the water quickly enough to spot the boat. The shooter was wearing all black. He's fit. A quick runner. I didn't get a good look at him, but I fired off two rounds. Between your shots and mine, he might've been hit. Deputies should alert the local hospitals."

Her body shook. An aftereffect of the adrenaline or from the intensity of the kiss, Laney couldn't tell. She brushed a lock of tangled hair from her eyes. Water dripped onto her lashes. The rain fell softly, and suddenly she felt the chill from her soaked clothing.

"Laney." Jonah stepped forward, his hand lifted as if he intended to touch her.

"Don't." Her voice was hard. Unyielding. Harsh.

He froze. A flash of devastation swept over his handsome features before he tucked it away.

She couldn't do this. If he touched her, she'd kiss him again, which would only make things worse. But she also couldn't take the hurt that would follow from this horrible mistake. "Let's just focus on the case, okay? We'll deal with this... later."

He was quiet for a long beat. "I'll call it in."

Laney nodded, and without looking at him, started the trek back to the cabin. Tears filled her eyes, and she battled them back. Her tennis shoes beat against the damp earth. Branches and briars tugged at her soaked pajamas, and she slipped on muddy patches. Her mind couldn't process anything that'd happened in the last half hour. Not the shooting or chasing the suspect.

Or the kiss. Definitely not the kiss.

Her cabin came into view. Bullet holes riddled the entire back side. The window on her back door and the one over her sink were busted. Laney raced up the porch steps. Inside was more chaos. Broken glass littered the floor. A bullet had slammed into her refrigerator. Another had broken the doggie cookie jar on her counter, shattering it.

Scout! She'd checked immediately after the shooting to ensure her dog was okay, but then she'd abandoned her to take off after the perpetrator. Stupid, stupid, stupid. Scout suffered from PTSD and reacted badly to flash bangs and gunfire. She must be terrified. On shaky legs, Laney crossed the kitchen. "Scout!"

The Labrador didn't bark, nor did she come running. A new wave of worry snapped her focus into place. Laney burst into the living room, her gaze sweeping the room in search of Scout. The dog wasn't there. Raindrops dripped off her pajamas and hair, leaving a trail of water in her wake as she headed for the bedroom. "Scout, sweetie, where are you?"

There was no sign of her dog. Her bed was empty, the frame too low for Scout to crawl under. Laney ran into the bathroom, searching, but Scout wasn't there. A wild thought struck her. Had there been two perpetrators involved? Had someone snuck into her house while she and Jonah were chasing the shooter and taken Scout? She couldn't fathom the reason for doing so, but then she also couldn't understand murder. Or unloading dozens of rounds on two members of law enforcement.

Laney raced back into the bedroom. In her panic and fear, she nearly missed the half-open closet door. Her pulse skyrocketed. She crossed the room in three strides, yanking the door open wide.

And her heart shattered.

Scout was balled up in a corner in the back of the closet. Her entire body trembled, and when she looked at Laney, her sorrowful brown eyes held sheer terror.

Laney dropped to the floor and wrapped her arms around her dog. "I'm here, sweetie. I'm here." Seeing Scout in such distress unlocked her own. Tears ran down her cheeks and dripped off her chin as she whispered words of comfort. Scout crawled into her lap. Gradually, the trembling subsided.

As her dog relaxed, Laney's own frantic thoughts settled. She stroked Scout's soft ears. Exhaustion set in as the adrenaline faded. For the first time, she could think clearly about what she'd done.

Chasing an armed suspect through the woods had been... reckless. Yes, she knew every tree and trail better than anyone, and yes, her fury at seeing Scout terrorized and Jonah threatened had driven her forward. But that hadn't justified her actions. She'd left her traumatized dog alone and put herself—and subsequently Jonah—in unnecessary danger. Jonah had been right to be angry with her.

She screwed up.

"I should have stayed with you," she whispered against Scout's fur. "I'm so sorry, girl."

Scout's answer was a kiss on her cheek. She nuzzled her dog, wishing they could stay hidden in the dark closet forever. A part of her wanted to be angry with Jonah. How could he have kissed her? What possessed him? But she was humble enough to see her part in it.

She'd kissed him back. Passionately. A momentary hormonal blip that had probably cost Laney her best friend. Because there was no going back. Oh, they'd built a friendship after dating for a month in college, sure. But back then, they hadn't had the foundation of a fifteen-year history. This time, things were different. The rejection would cut deeper.

And there would be rejection. There always was. Nothing lasted forever, and Laney always cut and ran before things got too real. Deep romantic connections were messy. Confusing. Heartbreaking. Jonah was a forever kind of guy. And she didn't believe in happily-ever-after.

Her mother hadn't gotten one. Why should Laney be any different?

The thought of going out there... of facing Jonah... she didn't know how she was going to handle it.

But she had to. Laney couldn't hide in the dark closet forever.

Gathering her courage, she pushed to her feet and, on rubbery legs, went into the bathroom. She washed her face, combed her hair, and pulled on a fresh ranger uniform. With her armor in place, Laney went back through the house and outside. In the fifteen minutes she'd been in the house, deputies had arrived. So had Ryker. He stood assessing the back of the cabin with Jonah.

And it was Jonah she couldn't tear her eyes away from.

Like her, he'd changed out of his wet clothes. A cowboy hat cast shadows over his eyes, and his sleeves were rolled up, revealing powerful forearms. She tried not to notice the way the fabric of his shirt stretched across his broad shoulders, tried not to remember how solid those muscles had felt under her hands.

This was Jonah. Her best friend. Her rock. The one person she could always count on through deployments, career changes, her mother's illness... everything.

She couldn't—absolutely refused—to think of him like this. Not if they stood any chance of salvaging their relationship.

As if he'd felt the call of her thoughts, Jonah's head swiveled toward her. His blue eyes locked on hers. She suddenly felt very warm and incredibly self-conscious. Ignoring the flare of heat in her cheeks, she squared her shoulders and forced her feet to move forward. Scout stayed at her side. The rain had lessened to a faint misty drizzle.

"Bad start to the morning," Laney joked as she drew closer, keeping her attention on Ryker. She purposefully kept from looking at Jonah, knowing that if she did, it would deepen her blush.

Gosh, this was so awkward. She wanted the earth to swallow her whole.

"You can say that again." Ryker gave her a brotherly one-armed hug. "Glad you're okay." He reached down to pet Scout. "All of you."

Laney's cabin looked like a slice of Swiss cheese. A tremble shook her insides as she gauged just how close she'd come to being shot. Jonah too. There was a concentration of bullets near the corner of the house where he'd taken cover. It was a miracle they all survived, and she sent up a prayer of thanks to the Good Lord. "Whoever did this wasn't messing around."

"No." Ryker's expression was grim. "Jonah said you chased the shooter through the woods."

Regret stabbed her. "It wasn't a smart move on my part, but yes. He knew exactly where he was going and had no trouble navigating the woods even at a full-on run. I didn't get a good look at him, but his boat was a silver dinghy with a black motor and rust spots along the left side. He took off westward." She paused. "Deputies were monitoring Garrett, right? So it couldn't have been him."

"Actually, it may have been." Ryker planted his hands on his hips but kept his voice pitched low to prevent the deputies who were stringing up crime scene tape from overhearing. "Chief Deputy Williams informed me that Garrett's lawyer demanded they remove the deputy sitting outside Garrett's house. He threatened them with a harassment lawsuit. She was forced to comply, but tried to manage the situation by having frequent patrols, but—"

"Garrett got past them," Jonah growled.

Ryker nodded. "He slipped out of his house this morning and hasn't shown back up yet. No one knows where he is."

What were the chances that Garrett evaded the deputies on the same morning her house was shot up? It could be a coincidence, but if so, it was an unlikely one.

Laney took note of the rabbit still hanging from her porch. Mindful of the crime scene and the broken glass, she ordered Scout to stay in the grass and then climbed the porch steps to take a closer look. The poor creature's neck had been broken, likely from being caught in an animal trap.

Be careful, little bunny. Be very careful.

"He used it to lure you outside."

Jonah's footsteps had been silent, and she jolted at the sound of his voice, so close to her. The hair on her arms rose as her pulse kicked up a notch. It felt like every cell in her body was attuned to him as he came to stand next to her. She kept her gaze on the rabbit, unwilling to look him in the eye. "Hunting and poaching in the park is illegal..." Her voice trailed off as a memory niggled.

"I doubt this guy cares about what's illegal. Killing wildlife is the least of his crimes—"

"The raccoon." She inhaled sharply as her mind connected a clue she hadn't known was important.

"Excuse me?"

"On the day that Ava and Tyler were killed, I came across a dead raccoon in a remote part of the park. The animal had been shot." She turned to look at her house.

The shooter had used a high-powered rifle. Different weapon, but he'd lost his handgun in the weeds near the lake while killing Ava. And most gun owners had more than one kind. "I forgot about the raccoon, but..." She gestured to the rabbit. "Maybe it's connected after all."

"Can you tell me where you found it?" Jonah asked, his voice carefully neutral. Professional. As if they were just colleagues discussing a case. As if he hadn't kissed her less than an hour ago.

Laney hesitated. Being alone with Jonah right now seemed like the worst possible idea. But they couldn't avoid each other forever, and they certainly couldn't solve this case without working together. If there was any way to save their relationship, they would have to talk about what happened. And that conversation... it needed privacy.

Bracing herself, Laney forced her gaze to meet his. "I'll take you there."

SEVENTEEN

Jonah held onto the handle over the door as Laney's SUV bounced over the rutted, gravel road. Trees towered over them, creating a canopy that shielded the weak sunlight filtering through the cloudy skies. The silence inside the cab was deafening. Loaded with unspoken words and unanswered questions. Jonah had always been an expert at reading Laney, but right now... he had no idea what she was thinking.

She'd kissed him back. He hadn't imagined that. The way her fingers had curled into his shirt, the desperation in the way she'd pulled him closer... She felt everything he did. She wanted it as much as he had. But the memory of Laney pushing him away, the fear in her eyes, told him everything he needed to know about where she stood.

He couldn't regret it, though. Fifteen years of buried emotion had finally broken through, and despite the mess they were in now, he couldn't bring himself to wish it hadn't happened. It'd been honest.

The question was what happened next. Laney ran from serious relationships as if they were a disease. She'd walk through actual fire to protect someone she cared about, but ask her to commit to a romantic relationship and she'd be halfway across the county before you finished the sentence. Would she run now? Or would she try to patch over what happened, pretend it was just adrenaline and fear?

He didn't want to lose her. He also didn't want to lie about his feelings anymore. If she just wanted to be friends, he'd live with that. But pretending he didn't love her? That option wasn't on the table any longer. He was done wasting time. Done pining for a woman who might never want the same thing he did.

Because in the end, that's what he'd been doing. He'd compared every woman to Laney, and they'd always come up short. He'd been holding out for her. The timing couldn't have been worse—they were in the middle of a homicide investigation and Laney's life was being threatened—but Jonah knew nothing short of seeing her in mortal danger could've shattered his careful restraint. It had taken the sight of those bruises on her neck, the sound of gunfire tearing through her cabin, to make him finally understand how easily she could be ripped from his life forever.

And suddenly, playing it safe wasn't the worst choice. Losing her without ever telling her the truth, never having the chance to know what might've been... that was the real risk he couldn't bear to take.

"We're here." Laney shoved the vehicle into Park and climbed out.

Jonah followed. Settling his cowboy hat on his head to ward off the persistent drizzle, he joined her and Scout next to the carcass of a raccoon. The smell of death permeated the air, mixing with the scent of pine and rain.

"When I found it, the kill was fresh. I remember thinking the poacher used a handgun to shoot the raccoon. A high-powered rifle would've obliterated it, and as you can see, the body was mostly intact. It was also done for sport." She tilted her head. "Which makes me wonder if our killer was practicing in these woods. He would've shot the raccoon hours before killing Ava and Tyler."

It was an interesting theory. "Tyler wasn't shot first. Nolan was."

"Yes, but Nolan was in an enclosed space. Inside a cabin. Tyler and Ava were camping out in the open. It's a lot harder to shoot a running target in the woods."

She had a point. "Let's collect the carcass for evidence. With any luck, the lab will recover the bullet and compare it to the ones that killed Tyler and Nolan. If the same gun was used on this raccoon and on the two men, then we know our killer is responsible for all of them."

His gaze settled on Laney. Raindrops gathered in her dark tresses, distracting him, reminding him too much of the kiss they'd shared. "It would be a good idea to stay somewhere else while the case is under investigation. The cabin is too exposed, too difficult to defend if the killer tries for you again. Ryker volunteered for us to stay with him and Hannah at their new house. It's a twenty-minute drive from here. Since Hannah is a district attorney, and after those threats against her a few years ago, he made it a priority to install the best security system money can buy."

"A security system won't stop a killer with a rifle, and I don't want to bring trouble to their doorstep. They've been through enough. Besides..." Her cheeks pinked, and she looked away. "They're newlyweds. They don't want houseguests."

"Somewhere else then—"

"No, I won't be scared off." She raised a hand to ward off his protest. "I'll move closer to the visitor center for the time being. There are a couple of free cabins over that way, near the mess hall. The sheer amount of foot traffic should provide some level of protection." Her jaw tightened. "Whoever this is only likes to strike when I'm isolated. I don't think he counted on you being at my cabin so early in the morning."

Her gaze skittered from his, and a flush rose in her cheeks. They hadn't done anything inappropriate. He'd slept on her couch more than once over the years, but on the heels of their passionate kiss, everything felt uncomfortable and loaded.

And... he didn't know what to say. So Jonah fell back on his training and focused on the case. He turned in a circle, assessing the surrounding woods. A trail ran through the trees. It was faint, but it was there.

Her attention landed on the raccoon, and a frown

creased her features. "You know, a perpetrator who can shoot a small animal like this with accuracy shouldn't have any issue taking out someone with a high-powered rifle, like the one used by the shooter this morning."

"Good point." Were they looking at two shooters? Maybe the raccoon wasn't connected at all? Still, Jonah would rather pursue the lead and find it went nowhere than dismiss it outright. He pointed to the faint trail. A worn-down wooden marker showed it was an official hiking path. "Where does that go?"

"Eventually it leads to the visitor center. We're in a remote section of the park, but we get some avid hikers out here on occasion. Let's see if it's been used recently."

She started for the path, followed by Scout. Jonah brought up the rear. For a while, their footsteps, Scout's panting, and the quiet patter of the rain filled the air. Occasionally, Laney would stop to assess a tree branch or some disturbed earth. He had the feeling she was looking for signs that someone had deviated from the path and gone farther into the woods.

"So... about this morning..." Laney sounded hesitant. "I'm sorry about running after the shooter. That wasn't smart, and you were right to be mad."

"I was scared. Not mad." It probably hadn't seemed that way since he'd been shouting. "I'm sorry for yelling at you. That was uncalled for, and unlike me."

She nodded and took a bracing breath. "And the kiss?"

"The kiss was..." A long time coming. A physical expression of everything he couldn't find the words to say. A demonstration of his love. None of those answers were anything Jonah felt he could utter out loud without sending Laney bolting. "...what it was."

She stopped to finger the leaf on a broken branch. Her voice dropped to a whisper. "I don't want to lose you, Jonah. We've been friends for fifteen years. That's not something I'm willing to risk over one impulsive moment."

"Is that what it was to you? Just an impulse?"

Her eyes widened. "Wasn't it for you?"

He could lie. Tell her that it was a moment of temporary insanity, that his feelings had overruled his head for one stupid moment. But Jonah was done being dishonest. With her. And with himself. "No, Laney. It wasn't an impulse." He paused, trying to figure out how to put what he'd realized into words. "I've had feelings for you for a long time, but I've never acted on them. It didn't seem like you felt the same way, and I didn't want to put our friendship at risk."

She swallowed. "How long?"

"What?"

"How long have you had feelings for me?"

"Since college, although they were less intense. And then you came to stay with me after I'd been injured in the line of duty. That's when I knew for sure."

She inhaled sharply. "That... that was eight years ago."

"Yes."

Her panic was palpable, and Laney took off at a fast clip down the hiking trail. Jonah hurried to catch up with her, his long strides eating up the distance between them, until he could lightly grab her arm and pull her to a stop. "Laney, just..." He drew in a breath and let it out slowly. "Look at me, Laney."

She shook her head, but he placed a finger under her chin and ever so gently lifted her face until her eyes met his. "Nothing has to change if you don't want it to. Do you understand? We can go back to being friends, and we'll never talk about this again."

Tears filled her eyes. "We can't go back."

"No, we just can't be dishonest anymore. You're my best friend. I have feelings for you, and I was too terrified to tell you." He swiped the wetness away from her cheek with his thumb. "If you don't feel the same way, then say so. I'll get over it. Move on. But..." He cupped her face. "You kissed me back, Laney. That has to mean something."

The fear in her gorgeous brown eyes broke him. Jonah pulled her into his arms. "I know you're scared. I won't pretend to understand all the reasons why, but it doesn't have to be this way. We can work through it. Just like we do everything else."

She held onto him with a desperation that was surprising, and then suddenly, Laney pushed away, swiping at the tears tumbling down her cheeks. "This is different."

There were only a few feet separating them, but it felt like an entire valley. His heart sank as her expression hardened before she turned away. Scout nudged Laney's hand, as if sensing her owner's turmoil and distress.

He'd spent years observing Laney's pattern with romantic relationships. Watched as she pulled back whenever someone got too close, ended things before they had a chance to develop. Over and over again. He'd never pushed her on it before, but this time was different. This time, it was about them.

"I'm not your dad, Laney."

Her shoulders stiffened. "I know that."

"Do you?"

The question hung in the air between them, and the searing hurt that followed caught Jonah off-guard with its intensity. He was nothing like Antonio Torres. Nothing. How could she not see that? Her denial had been quick and automatic, but they both knew it was a lie. Her dad— and the heartache he'd caused—stood between them as surely as if the man himself had been there.

And once again, as he had so many times in his life before, Jonah realized he wasn't good enough.

Laney sniffed. "I don't want to talk about this anymore right now. Can we just... table it until after the case is over?"

He wanted to say no. Wanted to tell her that they couldn't just shove this back in a box and pretend the lid was still sealed. But Laney was right. The murder case had to take priority. People's lives were at stake. His feelings, valid as they were, couldn't come before that.

Besides, pushing harder now would only drive her further away. "We'll table it. For now."

Relief flooded her features. "Thank you." Laney turned and continued down the path. The silence stretched between them, less awkward than before but no less potent. Jonah had a sinking feeling that whatever had just taken place would change their friendship forever. Maybe Laney was right, and there was no going back. He'd been a fool to think otherwise.

"Wait." Laney slid to a stop on the path.

She touched a broken branch and then eased off the trail into the trees. The tension in her shoulders sent a wave of concern running through him. Jonah placed his hand over the holster of his weapon. The ground was muddy, and the rain picked up from a drizzle to a persistent shower, drumming against the leaves overhead and running in rivulets off the back of Jonah's cowboy hat.

They entered a small clearing. A crude firepit ringed with blackened stones sat in the center. Flattened grass and holes in the ground indicated a tent had been pitched nearby. Scout sniffed the ground, her ears pricked forward. Laney placed her hands on her hips. "Someone was camping here illegally."

He didn't like this. "Can you tell how recently?"

She bent over the firepit, stirring the soaked ashes with a stick. "Until early this morning." She gestured to the holes in the ground. "Those were for his tent. The rain hasn't caused the dirt to fill in yet. We had thunderstorms last night, so they shouldn't be as visible as they are if he left before it rained."

Goosebumps rose on Jonah's arms. Suddenly, he realized just how vulnerable they were, standing there in the middle of the woods in the far reaches of the state park. He berated himself for being so stupid. If he hadn't been distracted by the kiss, and Laney's reaction, he might've thought twice about trekking around out here with a killer on the loose.

A branch snapped. Jonah whirled around, taking a protective stance in front of Laney, while pulling his weapon. His gaze scanned the thick foliage.

Behind him, Laney chuckled. "It's a deer, Foster. Relax."

He caught a flash of brown through the foliage and lowered his handgun. "We should get back to the car."

Laney had already pulled out her phone. "Let me get some pictures first. Keep an eye on Scout. She'll let us know if we have reason to be concerned." Laney winked, a teasing smile on her lips. "She ignores the deer."

"Yeah, yeah." His neck heated, but he couldn't shake the uneasy feeling plaguing him. He kept his handgun lowered but didn't bother holstering it. Once Laney was done documenting the illegal campsite, they traipsed back to the vehicle. The sight of the SUV untangled the nerves jittering his insides. Jonah finally holstered his weapon.

His phone rang with an incoming call. Tate. Jonah answered as he climbed into the passenger seat. "What's up?"

"I found something you need to see. I may know who our killer is."

EIGHTEEN

Thirty minutes later, Laney was sitting across from Tate. Beyond the closed door of the conference room, the phone at the front desk rang continuously. Reporters had caught wind of the shooting at her cabin, and on the heels of the murders, the story was slated to become national news. A media liaison was handling the official updates, but that didn't prevent reporters from calling the Piney Woods main phone number in an effort to get more information.

The pressure bearing down on her shoulders was compounding. The murder case, the superintendent job, the media... and now this mess with Jonah. A migraine was forming along the base of her skull. It didn't help that she couldn't stop noticing every time Jonah moved or even breathed. It was like the kiss had made her hyper-aware of him.

"I got to thinking last night." Tate's eyes were bright with excitement, but there were dark circles under them, which made Laney wonder if he'd even slept. "Someone like this is likely to have a criminal record. And we're dealing with a sex offender. So I asked Andy for a comprehensive list of everyone who volunteered here in the last year and started comparing them to the sex offender registry."

Jonah straightened. "You got a hit."

"Yep." With a triumphant look, Tate turned his laptop screen to face them. "Meet Mitch Caldwell."

Laney gasped. The recognition hit her immediately. She'd seen that lean face and stubby beard before. "That guy was here the other day. It's the fisherman I chased off."

Jonah slowly nodded. "The jumpy one." His expression hardened. "What was he convicted of?"

"He stalked and raped a young woman in Mississippi. She was a college student. Brown hair, brown eyes. He served five years. Mitch stayed in Mississippi and was complying with his parole requirements until six months ago. A warrant was issued for his arrest, but he skipped town. Deputies interviewed his mother. She swears she hasn't seen him, but get this, Mitch grew up here. Graduated from the local high school."

Her mouth fell open. "I don't understand. We conduct background checks on all of our volunteers. If Mitch is a registered sex offender, it should've shown up."

"That's the thing. When he filled out the official form, he used his older brother's name: Michael Caldwell. But when I ran Michael through our system, I discovered he was in the armed forces. Navy, to be exact. A quick phone call confirmed Michael was deployed during the Spring Jamboree. He couldn't have been volunteering here. Michael and Mitch are only one year apart in age, and they look enough alike to be twins. Michael Caldwell's record is clean, but Mitchell Caldwell is a registered sex offender."

"So he used his brother's legal name to pass the background check?"

"Yes. You provide free meals to your volunteers and pay them a small stipend during big events. I think that's why he volunteered during the Spring Jamboree. And I'll give you one guess where he was assigned."

Laney breathed out. "The wildlife center."

"Ding, ding, ding. He worked there all week. So, Mitch and Ava definitely crossed paths." Tate shuffled through the papers on the table before pulling out a photo. "This is the young woman Mitch assaulted. Notice anything?"

Laney took in the young woman's bright smile and her long brunette hair. Then, her gaze shot to the picture of Ava attached to the whiteboard. "They could be sisters." Her focus flickered to Lisa's photograph. Her eyes were hazel, but she also had brunette hair and a slender build. "Even Lisa is similar enough to fit the victim profile. Was Mitch's first victim involved with anyone?"

"No, she didn't have a boyfriend. But Mitch stalked her for months before he attacked her. And criminals can learn and adjust their methods."

Laney mulled that over. "Could Mitch have stalked Ava without her knowing?"

"It depends on how much he tried to interact with her. After going to prison, Mitch may have learned to keep his distance." Jonah frowned. "Ava was worried about Garrett. According to Kylie, he harassed her. Even if Ava had a sense that something wasn't right, she may have attributed anything weird to him."

He had a good point. An icy chill crept down Laney's back as a memory surfaced. "Brett mentioned that someone was in the lobby when Ava and Tyler checked in. A guy. He watched Ava intensely." She rose. "Do you have a printed photograph of Mitch Caldwell?"

"Yeah." Tate handed her one.

She went out into the lobby, Jonah on her heels. Brett was behind the front desk, helping a couple with a hiking trail reservation. Laney waited impatiently for him to finish. The continuous ringing of the phone was causing her migraine to bloom. She would need some caffeine, headache medicine, and food after this. The protein bar she'd choked down after the shooting had tasted like dust and done nothing to make her feel better.

She peeked at Jonah out of the corner of her eye. He watched Brett with the scrutiny of a man who didn't trust anyone. She had a sense he didn't like Brett, but she couldn't reason why. Truth be told, he didn't like Eddie either. Jonah had always been more cautious about people. It was one of the things she'd accepted about him but, at times, annoyed her. He tended to think the worst.

Laney had a laundry list of reasons why they

wouldn't work. She was a morning person. He couldn't stand being around anyone before noon. She loved to travel; he was a homebody. She believed God was actively involved in her daily life; he questioned why a loving God would allow so much suffering.

And yet... none of those differences had mattered when he kissed her. Or when he cupped her face, his touch so gentle she cried, and promised that nothing had to change unless she wanted it to.

If she was honest, her feelings for Jonah had been shifting for a long time. She'd fought against it. Hid it. Lied to herself about it. And at the same time, it'd been a shock to discover he'd been harboring romantic feelings for her for the last eight years. *Eight years*. She didn't know what to do with that.

Laney had no doubt Jonah cared for her, but that didn't mean he would feel the same way a year from now. Or ten years from now. People changed. They grew apart.

They left.

Jonah wasn't her dad. She knew that. But she doubted, on the day her parents got married, that her dad believed he would up and leave them eight years later. And Laney knew—without a doubt—if she allowed herself to fall in love with Jonah and then he fell out of love with her... she'd end up just like her mother. Crying years later over a wedding album, trying to figure out where it all went wrong.

She refused to allow anyone to have that power over her.

Even Jonah.

Finally, the couple left. Laney stepped up to the desk and greeted Brett with a polite smile. "We need your help. Do you recognize this man?" She turned the photo toward him.

A lock of sandy hair fell over his forehead as he studied Mitch's face. Then suddenly his eyes widened. "That's the guy who was staring at Ava. You found him?"

"Not exactly." Laney studied him carefully. "You're sure this is the guy?"

"100%. I remember his beard and that strange haircut." Brett's nose wrinkled. "It looks like he took a pair of scissors to his own hair and chopped away."

"Have you ever seen this man before that day with Ava?" Jonah asked. "Or since?"

Brett seemed to consider the question. Then he slowly shook his head. "Can't say I have."

"Okay. Thanks." Laney turned away, but Brett stopped her with a light hand on her arm. His expression when she faced him was earnest.

"Is there anything I can do to help with the investigation? I feel so responsible for what happened to Ava." He gestured to the photo in her hand. "Is that the guy who killed them?"

"He's a person of interest. If he comes into the lobby, or if you see him around the park, do not engage with him. Call me or Andy right away." She'd given this warning to Brett before but felt obligated to do so again. She didn't want him going rogue, searching for a killer in the park.

He hesitated and then nodded. "Yes, ma'am."

They headed back into the conference room. She filled Tate in on what Brett had said. Guilt stabbed her. Like Brett, she'd been within arm's reach of the killer and hadn't known it. Except she was a law enforcement officer with a duty to protect. Somehow, as illogical as it was, Laney felt as though she should've known better. She pictured Mitch again in her mind. His dirty clothes and unkempt appearance. His broken fishing pole.

She inhaled sharply. "He's the one camping illegally in the woods."

"What?" Tate asked, his brow furrowing.

She quickly ran through what they'd found, from the dead raccoon to the illegal campsite. "Mitch had the appearance of someone struggling to get by. He's wanted by law enforcement, so he can't go home, but he's close enough to his mother that he can meet her in secluded places in order to get supplies. He picked up the campsite, but I bet he's still around here somewhere." A thought tripped her up. "Where would Mitch get a boat?"

"He could've stolen it," Jonah offered.

"Yeah, but when we saw him, he was fishing in a restricted area. If he had access to a boat, doesn't it make more sense to use that instead?"

Jonah was quiet for a moment, his gaze distant as if he was thinking over her question. Then his expression darkened. His eyes shot to hers before flickering to the image of Mitch's first victim, then Lisa, and finally Ava. His entire body stiffened.

"What?" She instinctively grabbed his arm. The muscles were rigid underneath her palm, and the memory of their passionate kiss flashed unbidden in her mind. She quickly yanked her hand back.

Jonah's jaw tightened. No one else would've noticed the faint trace of hurt that curved his brow, but she did. A tangle of emotions roiled inside her, but she shoved them all back. Now was not the time to sort out the mess they were in. Instead, she kept her tone even and said, "You thought of something."

He nodded. And this time when he looked at her, there was worry clouding his blue eyes. "You look like them."

"Like who—" She froze. Slender brunettes. Athletic. Outdoorsy. Laney blinked, her mind unwilling to lump herself in with the other women. "But that's... that can't be why he's after me. It doesn't make sense. He tried to shoot me this morning. Ava and Lisa were both strangled."

"Maybe his intention was to kill Jonah." Tate leaned back in his chair. "He kills the boyfriend in front of the woman, and then he attacks her. You're a law enforcement officer. He's going to be more cautious with you. Take less risk."

Laney's heart beat against her rib cage. The killer coming after Jonah? She couldn't think of it. Somehow during the shooting and the aftermath, it hadn't even occurred to her to think about the fact that Jonah could've died. Her fingers trembled. "But we're not together."

Tate's brows rose. "Sorry to tell you this, Laney, but if I didn't know you guys were just friends, I'd think you were dating. The casual touches, the way you laugh and joke with each other... your closeness is obvious. I don't think the killer picked you out initially, but after you escaped that first night, I could see it happening. You resemble the other victims and would be a challenge." He shrugged. "Jonah would be collateral damage. Just like Tyler and Nolan."

A coldness centered in Laney's chest like a block of ice. She could handle danger. Had walked into it more than once during her career with the military. And she knew Jonah could handle himself, but it was terrifying to think his proximity to her, his relationship with her, had made him a target.

"That's enough, Tate." Jonah shot him a dirty look. "Let's not speculate. Focus on what we know. For starters, we need to find Mitch Caldwell. If he's truly living in the far reaches of the park, then we need to conduct a search for him. That'll take manpower we don't have at the moment. Let's request it."

Focus. Focus on the case, not on the fear clawing her insides.

She drew in a breath. "We should distribute his photograph to my rangers, and alert them that someone may be camping illegally in the park. They're patrolling in pairs for safety and can keep an eye out for anything suspicious."

"Good idea." Jonah checked his watch. "Ryker was following up with Chief Deputy Williams about Garrett

Wheeler. I'd like to know if he's reappeared yet. We also need to check on Eddie Sorenson's restraining order. I'll find his ex-wife. Let's see what she has to say about her ex-husband's temperament."

Laney swung toward Jonah. "You still think Eddie might be responsible for this?"

"Right now, I'm not eliminating anyone unless they have a rock-solid alibi." He held her gaze. "Mistakes can be deadly, Laney, and I refuse to let anything else happen to you."

She swallowed hard. Laney knew without a doubt that Jonah would do anything for her. A terrifying realization. What had Tate called it? Collateral damage.

Would protecting her cost Jonah his life?

NINETEEN

Mitchell Caldwell was a ghost. Garrett Wheeler was still missing. And Jonah...

Well, he was irritated, frustrated, and annoyed in equal measure. "Tate should've kept his big mouth shut about the killer coming after me. It completely freaked Laney out." He glowered out the vehicle window. The afternoon sunshine was hidden behind a new wall of clouds. More rain was coming. It was as if God intended to cure the entire summer's drought in the span of a few days. "She's got enough to worry about. I don't want her trying to protect me on top of it."

Ryker shot him a baleful look. "You don't think Laney would've put two and two together?"

"Eventually, sure. But Tate spelled it out for her." His jaw clenched. "The one time he decides to actually speak his mind..."

"Tate was speaking to two law enforcement professionals, one being the acting superintendent for the park.

Laney deserves to know what's going on, and she's not a delicate violet who needs to be coddled and protected. She's tough enough to handle the truth."

Ryker's logic only irritated Jonah further. "It was an asinine thing to say. He called me collateral damage, for heaven's sake, so stop sticking up for him."

"Something tells me you're mad at something other than Tate."

"No, I'm pretty ticked at him."

Ryker tapped his finger on the steering wheel. "Sure. That's why you left him back at the park to watch over Laney."

She had to stay back and prepare for the upcoming meeting with the representatives from TDPW tomorrow. Jonah hadn't been happy about it, but Tate was reliable enough to keep her alive. Even if he couldn't keep his mouth shut. "I hope he doesn't say something else that he shouldn't."

The truck rolled to a stop at a red light. Ryker shifted to face Jonah. "What's going on between you and Laney?"

"Nothing. We're fine."

Ryker snorted. "You're both as tense as rookies on their first day."

He rolled his eyes. "We were shot at this morning."

"That's not it, and we both know it. You could barely look at each other this morning. I've never seen either of you so uncomfortable, so let's skip through your denials and my pushing. Just start talking, Foster."

He debated ignoring his friend, but what would be

the point? Besides, he could use someone to talk to. "I kissed her. She kissed me back. And now it's awkward." He glowered out of the window as the light turned green and they moved through the intersection. "Laney's never been great with romantic relationships. They freak her out. And like a world-class moron, I told her I've had feelings for her for the last eight years. So... now you know."

"You think Laney doesn't care?"

"Oh, I know she cares. That's not an issue." She'd kissed him back. Jonah knew that meant something. "But she's scared."

"Of what?"

"I don't know exactly." He flexed his fingers. "Her dad abandoned the family when Laney was eight. She doesn't talk about it much. Maybe it has something to do with that? I don't know. But if it does, it sucks that she hasn't figured out that I'm not like that. We've been friends for fifteen years. You'd think that would count for something."

Ryker was silent for so long Jonah thought the conversation was over, and then he said, "Hannah fought her feelings for me too. When a woman's been hurt before, it can be hard for her to risk her heart again." He flicked a glance toward Jonah. "Whatever Laney's going through, I doubt it has anything to do with you, and everything to do with her."

Jonah wasn't so sure about that, but he was willing to listen. "So what do I do?"

"Be patient. Stay steady. Give her the space and time to sort out her heart."

"Have faith, you mean." He'd never been very good at that. Surrendering to God felt so... passive. He preferred taking action and making things happen. Or in this case, fixing what he'd broken.

But there was no fixing it. No going back.

"Sometimes it takes more strength to stand steady," Ryker said. "And if you want my opinion, it sounds like Laney needs you now more than ever. She's in turmoil. Everything she thought about you and your relationship has been turned upside down. That's bound to make anyone nervous, especially if Laney's always struggled with commitment. But you've built fifteen years of trust with her. Have faith that she'll find her way."

It was no small task. Already Jonah felt Laney was putting up walls between them. And it hurt.

Ryker pulled into a popular fast-food restaurant and parked his truck. "Come on, let's see if Eddie's ex will talk to us. It would be nice to knock at least one primary suspect off our list today."

They found Georgia Parker enjoying a smoke break next to a sour-smelling dumpster. Her sallow yellow uniform gave her complexion a more ashen color than seemed possible. Dyed black hair was tucked into a hair-net, and wrinkles deepened near her lips as she puckered to draw in a cloud of smoke and nicotine.

"Why do you want to talk to me about Eddie?" Georgia eyed them with suspicion. "We've been divorced for years."

"We're gathering information," Jonah said carefully, "and we saw you took out a restraining order against

Eddie before your divorce was final. What can you tell us about that?"

She scrutinized him with the flat cold eyes of someone who didn't trust law enforcement. "I can tell you it's ancient history." Georgia tapped some ashes onto the ground. "Look, if you're interested in finding out information about Eddie, talk to him. I got nothin' nice to say about him, but our marriage was a mistake from the start. And I ain't interested in helping the police bulldoze anyone."

She tossed her cigarette onto the ground and rose. Jonah put out his hands in a placating manner. "Please, ma'am. We're not looking to bulldoze anyone. All we want is the truth." He paused, praying she could see his sincerity. "It's important."

She crossed her arms over her chest. "Is this about the murders at the park? It's all over the news."

He sensed Georgia wouldn't appreciate dishonesty, so he nodded. "It is."

"And you think Eddie could be involved?"

"I'm interested in hearing what you think."

Her gaze narrowed. "My ex is a cheater and a liar. He has a dark side." She gestured vaguely to her face. "I learned that the hard way. But if you're asking if he's a killer? The answer is no."

"Men willing to hit women are often capable of much worse."

She let out a laugh that dissolved into a cough. "Eddie's not that smart. He couldn't even hide his mistresses from me. Notice I said mistresses. Plural." Her nose wrinkled with disgust. "I should've left him a long time before I did, but I wanted to make the marriage work. I was a fool back then."

Ryker's expression was sympathetic. "It can be hard when the person you love doesn't honor their vows. You describe him as a cheater and a liar. He hit you. How can you be certain he's not involved in these murders?"

"Because I am. Listen, I have to get back to work—"

"Wait. One more second of your time." Jonah wasn't quite ready to give up. Eddie was hiding something. He was certain of it. Mitch had volunteered for the Spring Jamboree and worked alongside Ava. Which meant Eddie had been his supervisor. On a whim, Jonah unlocked his phone and pulled up a picture of Mitchell Caldwell. "Do you recognize this man?"

Georgia's eyes widened. "That's a buddy of Eddie's. They went to high school together. Mitch something or other." A visible shudder rippled through her. "Now that guy... he's bad news. Downright creepy. He has this way of looking at you... no, through you. Like he's undressing you with his eyes. It's gross."

"Have you seen him recently?"

"No. He and Eddie lost contact with each other a while ago. I only met Mitch a few times, the last being..." She tilted her head. "Must've been five or six years ago. Maybe more. It's been a long time." Georgia checked her watch and then smoothed her apron. "I gotta get back or my boss will have my hide."

"Thanks for your time."

She disappeared back inside the restaurant. Jonah

waited until they were back on the road before saying, "I knew Eddie was hiding something. He must've known Mitch was camping illegally in Piney Woods. Probably even knows he's the one behind the murders." His hands balled into fists. "Nothing should surprise me anymore, I know, but the ability of people to cover for killers... it angers me every time."

"We can't jump to that conclusion yet. Eddie hasn't been asked about Mitchell. He wasn't at work today."

"Then let's pay him a home visit."

Jonah pulled up the address and plugged it into the vehicle's GPS. Ten minutes later, Ryker pulled up to a small redbrick house with an overgrown front yard. The garage door was open. Eddie was hunched over a motor- cycle that'd seen better days. Numerous parts littered the cement. He straightened as they approached, his expres- sion blanching. Why did the man always look guilty every single time they spoke?

Ryker whistled as he approached. "Is that a '68 Triumph Bonneville?"

Eddie's brows winged up in surprise. "You know your bikes."

"My stepfather and I restored a few." Ryker's mouth hitched as he rubbed a loving hand over the torn leather seat. "My stepdad never rode them because my mom wouldn't allow it. Too dangerous, she said, and secretly, I think he agreed. But some of our best times together were the hours spent in the garage tinkering around."

"My dad loved motorcycles." Eddie's expression

grew sad and pensive. "We were supposed to restore this one together and never got around to it before he passed."

"I'm sorry. That's tough. But boy, she's gonna be a beauty when you're done with her."

Ryker bent down to examine some scrap of metal and spent the next few minutes talking about carburetors. Taking the hint, Jonah hung back, letting his colleague take the lead. He could already see a connection building between the two men, and that would only encourage Eddie to open up.

Finally, Ryker shifted the conversation to the case. He pulled up a photo of Mitchell on his phone. "Hey, man, I'm hoping you can help us out. Do you know this guy?"

"That's Mitch. Mitchell Caldwell. We went to high school together." Eddie frowned. "Why are you asking about Mitch? Last time I heard, he was in prison for stalking and attacking some woman..." His eyes widened. "Oh wait, you... Mitch is here? In town?"

"His mom denies it, but Mitch has been spotted in the park. We also found evidence that someone is camping illegally in Piney Woods." Ryker's tone was friendly, but his gaze sharp. "You haven't seen Mitch hanging around, have you? He hasn't contacted you?"

Eddie shook his head. "I don't mess with the likes of people like Mitch anymore."

"We spoke to your ex. She didn't have nice things to say about Mitch."

He looked surprised, and then it faded into resignation. "I'm sure she didn't. Georgia always hated him. Rightfully so, as it turned out."

"She said you and Mitch were friends in high school."

"We were." He was quiet for a long moment, his eyes shooting to Jonah. Redness formed along the back of his neck. "Look, I haven't been completely honest with you. But I need to know that the two of you will keep what I say between us." He met Jonah's gaze. "I don't want to lose my job."

"That's not a promise I can make. What I can say is that our interest is in finding a killer." Jonah let some sympathy bleed into his voice. "Laney's not unreasonable. She clearly isn't looking to fire you, so if I were you, I'd be honest and we'll see what happens after that."

Eddie seemed to mull that over and then sighed. "Yes, Mitch and I used to know each other in high school. I was something of a wild child back then. When my dad was diagnosed with Parkinson's, it was a wakeup call. My mom died when I was a kid, and my dad was all I had. I straightened up, got my GED, and went to community college." He leaned against the workbench behind him. "Shortly after starting at Piney Woods, I met Georgia. We fell in love fast and hard. But there were problems from the start. She'd had a tough childhood, and somehow, I had it in my mind that I could save her. As you can imagine, that didn't go well.

"My dad was getting sicker and sicker. My marriage was on the rocks." Eddie swallowed hard. "I started drinking and was a functional alcoholic for several years, but when my dad died last spring, things spiraled out of control. I could hold it together at work somewhat, but not well. I was late often, my work was sloppy. Most of my memories from that time are a blur. That's why I didn't recall Ava at all."

Jonah was curious about where this was going. He nodded to show he was still listening.

"Then I had a fight with Georgia. I didn't lie about what happened. I did accidentally hit her, but I was pretty drunk and not in the best frame of mind. The restraining order she took out against me was the wakeup call I needed. I stopped drinking the next day and put myself in AA." He hooked his thumbs in his pockets. "I did lie about where I was on the night Ava and Tyler were murdered. I was at an AA meeting."

"Where was the meeting held?"

Eddie gave the name of a local church and included his sponsor's contact information. "I was also there on the night Nolan and Lisa were murdered. I had nothing to do with their deaths."

"Why didn't you just say so?" Jonah asked.

"I didn't want Laney to find out. I love my job, and I'm afraid that if she knew how long I'd been working drunk..." Eddie swallowed hard. "People gave me a pass last spring because they thought I was grieving my dad. And I was. But if they knew I'd been drunk... they'd treat me differently."

"Not Laney." Jonah knew that with certainty. "You could've told her privately. She would've kept your secret."

"Yes, but she'd also be looking for any sign that I'd fallen off the wagon. I don't want that." Eddie shifted his boot-clad feet. "I'm only telling you now because it's clear you suspect me of something. I didn't have anything to do with these murders. If Mitch is in town, he hasn't contacted me. And I hope he never does. That chapter of my life is over."

Jonah studied the other man for a long beat. Eddie met his gaze without wavering. He was still fidgety, fiddling with his belt loops constantly, but it seemed more of an absentminded gesture.

Still, Jonah wasn't ready to completely buy his story yet. "Would you be surprised to learn that Mitch worked as a volunteer at the Spring Jamboree? He was at the wildlife center with Ava. You would've supervised them both. Are you telling me you didn't recognize your high school buddy?"

Eddie blinked. "He what?" He straightened. "No, he didn't. Michael Caldwell did. That's Mitch's older brother."

"No, it wasn't. Michael Caldwell was deployed during the Spring Jamboree."

Jonah let the silence stretch out. It took a couple of beats for Eddie to connect the dots.

His mouth dropped open, and he gaped like a fish pulled from a stream. His hands shot up, palms facing Ryker and Jonah. "I didn't know. I swear it."

Jonah's gaze narrowed. "Mitch didn't say anything?"

"No, and I had no reason to doubt it. He and Michael look like twins." Eddie dropped his hands. "Again, I wasn't in a great headspace back then, and I was drinking. Maybe now I might've realized, but back then..." He shook his head. "It didn't even occur to me."

"Do you think it's possible Mitch is guilty of the murders?" Ryker asked.

Eddie hesitated. "Mitch was never the sharpest knife in the drawer. I guess it's possible, but..." He shrugged. "Maybe? He was smart enough to use his brother's name. I could see him camping illegally in the park, though. Especially if he needed to hide out somewhere."

"Can you think of anyone Mitch would contact if he needed help?"

"His mom." Eddie thought for a moment longer. "Garrett Wheeler, maybe."

"Garrett." Jonah straightened. "How do Garrett and Mitch know each other?"

Eddie's focus jumped back to Jonah. "Mitch and I both worked for Garrett's company for a while. Mostly grunt work, like answering phones and organizing equipment, but he taught us a lot about surviving in the woods. Most of my knowledge about Piney Woods came from hiking with him. Garrett and Mitch were pretty close. Mitch worked for Garrett a lot longer than I did, and... well, they're birds of a feather."

"What does that mean?"

"My ex-wife had her faults, but she was always a pretty good judge of character. She didn't like Garrett any more than she liked Mitch. She categorized both of them as creepy. Her word, not mine."

"You hung out with them both too. How would you describe them?"

"Ranger Foster, I think we've concluded from this conversation that I'm the absolute worst judge of character. I'm a recovering alcoholic and a coward who refuses to tell the truth to my boss about my failings because I'm afraid of what she'll think." Eddie blew out a breath. "Garrett and Mitch talked about women as if they were objects. In my misguided youth, I did the same. Now... thinking back on some things they said... it makes me sick."

Jonah's phone buzzed with a text message. While Ryker asked a follow-up question, he glanced at the screen. It was from Chief Deputy Williams.

We found Garrett Wheeler. He's refusing to talk, and his lawyer is on the way to the sheriff's department.

He paused, his fingers over the tiny keyboard. So far, Garrett's lawyer had refused to allow him to answer questions.

But maybe... maybe... there was a way to change that.

TWENTY

Laney hit Save on the document and pushed away from her desk. Hours of preparation for the upcoming meeting with the Texas Department of Parks and Wildlife had left her muscles aching. Andy looked equally ready for a break.

"I think we have it." She rose and gave her second-in-command a high-five. It hadn't been easy to categorize and prioritize all the renovations and programs they wanted to accomplish in the next year, but she thought they had a good plan. "Thanks for helping."

Andy smiled, flashing his crooked bottom tooth. "It's my job." He gathered his file folders. "By the way, I contacted the volunteers who worked in the wildlife department from the Spring Jamboree. The consensus on Eddie was that he seemed not to care much. Several people remembered Ava, but didn't have anything significant to say, other than she seemed like a sweet young lady. No one recalled her having an issue with anyone, including Mitchell/Michael Caldwell."

Disappointment pinched. "It was worth a try."

He nodded. "In the meantime, Mitchell's photo has been distributed to all the rangers. Several reported seeing him on the park grounds at various times off and on since the Spring Jamboree. It doesn't seem like he's camping here permanently. I suspect he may only do so when he doesn't have any other place to crash or is worried that law enforcement is on to him."

"You're probably right." She couldn't imagine living in the woods during the miserable Texas summer when the heat and humidity made it almost unbearable. Then again, a criminal wanted by law enforcement might do almost anything to escape detection.

But why kill two couples? Did Mitch really believe he wouldn't be caught? Even so, attacking Laney... shooting at her cabin... that would only bring more law enforcement to the park. He'd spent so much time hiding, it seemed illogical to do things that might expose him.

A knock on her doorframe interrupted her thoughts. Tate popped his head in. "Sorry to interrupt, but Jonah called. Garrett Wheeler has been located and is down at the sheriff's department waiting for his lawyer. He says we should head that way."

"Of course." Laney whistled for Scout and grabbed her keys. She said goodbye to Andy and then hurried out into the late afternoon. Wind blew through the trees, and drizzle dampened her hair. When Tate headed for his vehicle, she lightly touched his arm. "Can we take mine? It has a crate in the back for Scout's safety."

"Of course."

Tate followed Laney to her vehicle, and moments later, they were headed for the sheriff's department. Country music softly played from her speakers. Her mind whirled with the knowledge that Garrett had been found. "Do we know where Garrett has been all day?"

"Jonah didn't say." Tate shifted uncomfortably in his seat. "Listen, Laney, I'm sorry about what I said during our meeting earlier. About Jonah being collateral damage. That was a foolish comment, one I said without considering how it would make you feel—"

"Don't apologize. What you said was the truth." She shot him a reassuring smile. "And it was something I would've figured out on my own. Don't let Jonah's bad attitude convince you that you did something wrong. He's just a grump, which I'm sure you've already figured out from working with him."

Tate chuckled. "Still, I could've been more sensitive." He paused. "You care a lot about him, don't you? Jonah?"

"We've been friends for a long time."

Friends. Such a simple word, but the weight felt so different now. What she felt for Jonah went far beyond mere friendship. Her lips still tingled with the heat of his kiss, but she had to bury these troublesome feelings and romantic notions. It was the only way forward. A thought she convinced herself was absolutely possible.

That was until she stepped into the conference room at the sheriff's department and saw him.

Jonah stood at the front of the room. His hair was windblown, and a five o'clock shadow darkened his jaw. His shirt was the color of a bluebird sky and matched his eyes perfectly. The first button was undone, revealing the curve of his throat. When had she ever found that section of skin attractive on a man?

The shirt had been a gift from Laney for his birthday last year, along with a leather-bound journal she'd found during a rare outing to an antique store. The sight of him wearing it did funny things to her insides. She forced herself to act natural while greeting everyone else. Ryker was there, along with Chief Deputy Williams.

Jonah waved toward some chairs. "Perfect timing, guys. Sit. I was just about to hand over the meeting to Special Agent Emilia Knox with the Texas Department of Public Safety's Criminal Investigations Division. She has some insight to provide us about our killer."

Laney claimed a seat, Scout settling at her feet, as Emilia rose. She nodded and smiled at Laney, and Laney returned the kind gesture with a slight wave. The two women were friends and had met several times socially. Emilia was one of the most compassionate people Laney had ever met. She'd often wondered if the horrific incident Emilia had experienced at the hands of a serial killer had made her more passionate about her cases or if she'd always been that way.

Jonah took a seat next to Laney. The scent of his laundry detergent layered with peppermint breath mints washed over her, and she felt her muscles inexplicably relax. She knew Garrett was somewhere in the building.

Laney hadn't realized how tense that made her until she felt Jonah's reassuring and protective presence at her side.

"I've reviewed the case files for both murders and created a profile of your killer." Emilia brushed a strand of her dark hair away from her face. "This should not be considered an exact or comprehensive list of traits. This is just something to guide you as you interview persons of interest. You are looking for someone between the ages of 30-45. Organized. Methodical. He probably lives alone but appears to others as friendly and outgoing. He could be in a romantic relationship, but if so, his partner will be subservient to him. The perpetrator likes control. He planned the murders carefully, but judging from what I saw in Nolan and Lisa's murders, I don't think he has killed before now."

"What makes you say that?" Chief Deputy Williams asked.

"Because he hesitated after shooting Nolan, for starters. Long enough, Lisa could crouch down next to Nolan and provide first aid before being forced to run away. There were signs even during the killer's attack on her that he was uncertain."

"Do you think that Lisa and Nolan were practice for Tyler and Ava?" Jonah asked.

"I think it's possible. The killer was focused on Ava, spent more time with her. But that could simply be because he'd already murdered once and was more comfortable." Emilia frowned. "What I will say is that the perpetrator is cautious. That's what makes me think he's older."

"What about prior crimes?"

"He may not have any. A criminal like this will be described by his exes as controlling, manipulative, and arrogant. Smart too. He is probably abusive toward them, but not necessarily physically. It could be emotional and mental abuse." She strolled to her spot at the table on impossibly high heels and opened her leather-bound notepad. "I've reviewed your known suspect list. The ones that best fit the profile are Eddie Sorenson and Garrett Wheeler."

Laney leaned forward. "What about Mitch Caldwell? He's a known stalker and rapist."

"I would never tell you to eliminate him from the suspect list based on my profile, but in my opinion, Mitch is too impulsive to have pulled off this crime. At least, he used to be." Emilia's pert nose wrinkled. "In his previous case, Mitch was brazen about his stalking. Amateurish. But he also went to prison for six years and may have learned a thing or two from other criminals. He's also older and may have more self-control now too. It's hard to say without interviewing him."

Frustration built in her chest. "No one has seen him at the park since I chased him away from the lake the other day for fishing in the wrong area."

"I've got deputies patrolling his mother's neighborhood." Chief Deputy Williams raised a pen. "No sign of him there either. The state police are sending a search unit on Wednesday morning. We'll comb through the isolated part of Piney Woods for both Mitch and any evidence, including areas he may have camped in. Where do we stand with Eddie Sorenson?"

"Jonah and I interviewed him this afternoon."

Ryker ran through the chain of events starting with Eddie's ex and then Eddie. When he got to the part about Eddie being in AA, shock vibrated through Laney. She hadn't had an inkling about his drinking problem last spring.

"We've spoken to Eddie's sponsor and the pastor of the church, who confirmed Eddie was there for an AA meeting from 7:15 to about 8:00 on Wednesday and Thursday," Ryker continued. "However, it's still possible he committed the murders. Tyler was shot at 9:15, according to the fireworks complaint that was called in."

Jonah nodded. "It only takes forty minutes to drive from the church where the AA meeting took place to Piney Woods. He would've had time to spare."

"But he had to pick up the Jeep Cherokee from wherever he stored it," Laney pointed out. "After killing Nolan and Lisa, the perpetrator stole their vehicle in order to use it the following night when he killed Ava and Tyler. So forty minutes to drive to Piney Woods, another ten to switch vehicles and another ten or fifteen to drive to Campsite 8. That's cutting it pretty close."

"The vehicle hasn't been found yet, and we can't be certain Eddie didn't hide it on a back road in Piney Woods. He could've driven straight to it, changed vehicles and then continued on to Campsite 8. We can time it, but I'm almost sure Eddie could've pulled it off." Ryker tilted his head. "But I have to say, I was convinced that he's telling the truth. Both his sponsor and the pastor said he's mild-mannered and not prone to anger. Even his ex said she didn't think he was capable of committing the murders."

"So we keep him on the suspect list, just in case, but we shift our focus." Chief Deputy Williams frowned. "What about Garrett Wheeler? He fits Emilia's profile and claims he was home alone during both nights of the murders. He's cooling his heels in Interview 1, but I can guarantee his lawyer won't let him talk to us."

"Did he mention where he's been all day?" Laney asked. The shooting at her cabin happened this morning, but it felt like years since then.

"Nope. He willingly came down here but insisted on waiting for his lawyer." She checked the smartwatch on her wrist. "Who should be here any moment."

"Good, because I have an idea that might get Garrett talking." Jonah leaned forward. "Let's show him Mitch's picture. I think Garrett knows his buddy is camping illegally in Piney Woods. If we make it seem like we're looking at Mitch for the murders, maybe Eddie too, and all we want is Garrett's help—"

Laney smiled. "Then he may talk to us. Brilliant idea."

His gaze met hers. "I'm glad you think so. Because I'm gonna need your help to sell it. Garrett doesn't like me very much, but he certainly has a soft spot for you. Ready to play good cop/bad cop again?"

TWENTY-ONE

Jonah wasn't convinced it was a good idea to include Laney in the interview, but he was certain Garrett would refuse to speak to him alone. Or with another Ranger. They had only one shot at this and needed to make it count. Still, when Garrett's gaze clapped on Laney as they walked into the room, a shudder of revulsion rippled through him, and it took every ounce of training to ignore the instinctive urge to protect her.

"Hello, Garrett." Laney's voice was soft, her smile bordering on flirtatious. "Thanks so much for coming down to talk to us."

"I wasn't given much of a choice." His eyes flickered toward Jonah, and his lip curled.

Jonah thought a lot of uncharitable things but kept his expression neutral and unbothered. There might be a time to turn on his "bad cop", but it wasn't at the beginning of the interaction. Instead of sitting at the table, he leaned against the far wall. His posture was relaxed and non-threatening, but he was close enough to Laney to come to her aid, if need be.

Discreetly, he assessed Garrett. The man was dressed much as he had been the first time they met, in a moisture-wicking shirt and utility pants. His boots had fresh mud clinging to the soles. He wore a sports watch, and a backpack rested in a corner of the room. A thermal water bottle poked out from one pocket.

"I'm sorry." Laney pulled out a chair and sat. "We've had some developments in the case, and we could use your help. I was hoping you could answer a few questions for us. Before we get started, can I offer you anything? Coffee? Water? A soda?"

"I'd like a Diet Coke—"

"We won't be here long enough for you to drink it." His attorney placed a hand on Garrett's arm. The lawyer's thinning gray hair was slicked back from a mousy-looking face, and his tie shimmered in the fluorescent lighting. "My client will not answer any questions, and if the sheriff's department and Texas Rangers don't stop harassing him, I'm going to sue all of you."

Laney kept her expression serious, but understanding. "I'm sorry, Mr..."

"Randall. Paul Randall." He sniffed, as if annoyed she hadn't recognized him.

"Mr. Randall, I can appreciate how protective you are of your client, but before you leave, I'd like to ask you to hear me out. Then you and Garrett can decide whether you're willing to help us." Laney opened the file folder she'd brought in with her and pulled out a blown-up driver's license photograph of Mitchell Caldwell. "Currently, we're looking for this man. He's a known stalker and rapist. Horrible case." She visibly shuddered as if she couldn't bear to think of it. Then her focus locked on Garrett. "I was hoping you could help us find him. His name is Mitchell Caldwell, but you may know him as Mitch."

He glanced at the picture and recognition flared in his eyes. "Why are you looking for Mitch?"

"We think he might be involved in the murders. We're hoping to learn more about him, and since he worked for you for a time, I think you could be very helpful."

"So... my client isn't here as a suspect?" Paul squinted as if trying to figure out Laney's endgame.

She smiled. "Mr. Randall, I represent the Texas Department of Parks and Wildlife. The sheriff's department and the Texas Rangers may view Garrett as a person of interest, but if you help me today, then I'm sure we can convince them that your client has nothing to do with these awful crimes. After all, we all want the same thing. The killer behind bars."

Jonah pressed his lips together at the placating tone in her voice. She should've gone into acting. Little did Paul or Garrett know, Laney's sweet demeanor hid a wickedly smart mind.

Garrett leaned over and whispered in his attorney's ear. Paul smoothed a hand over his tie. "I'd like to confer with my client in private for a moment."

"Of course. I'll use that time to get you a Diet Coke, Garrett. Mr. Randall, can I offer you anything?"

"A water would be appreciated."

"Sure thing." Laney rose gracefully. "Just give a holler when you're ready for me to come back in. I'll be right in the hall."

Jonah followed her out and made sure the door shut firmly behind them. Then he grinned at her and whispered, "You played that perfectly."

"We got their interest, that's for sure."

Tate appeared at the end of the hall, Scout by his side. He juggled a few drinks, including a Diet Coke and a bottle of water. "I didn't know what you'd like, Laney, so I grabbed a couple of options. Probably best if you drink something along with them."

She patted Scout and then said, "Give me a Diet Coke."

Jonah's brow wrinkled. "You hate Diet Coke... oh, you smart little vixen. You're using Emilia's profile to your advantage."

The killer wanted a subservient partner. Laney was playing right into that, making herself seem agreeable and deferential. Someone Garrett would feel superior to.

Jonah shook his head in admiration. "You're letting him think he's in control of the situation. By mirroring his drink, you're on the same team. Subtle, but effective."

She batted her eyelashes. "I'm just a pliable, innocent female who needs a big strong man to help me solve my case." Laney leaned over and peeked in the small window cut into the door of Interview 1. "Oh, the lawyer's getting up. Shoo, Tate. Scout, go with Tate, girl."

The lab hesitated and then trotted behind Tate and disappeared with him into the viewing room. Ryker, Chief Deputy Williams, and Emilia were all observing the interview from there. Cameras caught several angles of the interview room and were controlled remotely. They couldn't be on when Garrett was speaking to his attorney since those conversations were protected by privilege, but for the rest of the time, the cameras were active.

The interview room door opened, and Paul greeted them with a nod. "We're ready for you."

"Great." Laney made the word sound breathless, as if she couldn't quite believe her luck that Garrett had agreed to talk to her.

She hurried back inside the room. Jonah followed more slowly, keeping his expression neutral, and retook his position against the wall. This time, Garrett ignored him. His attention was locked on Laney as she offered him a Diet Coke before popping her own open. "I just love these." She laughed lightly. "Probably drink far too many of them, if I'm honest."

"Same." Garrett flexed his forearm muscle before popping open his own soda.

Jonah's stomach turned. He wanted to haul Laney out of the room, as far away from this... this creep as possible. It wasn't just professional suspicion. Something about the way Garrett looked at women, especially Laney, set off every protective instinct Jonah had.

Even if Garrett wasn't their killer, he wasn't a good man.

He listened to Laney jabber on about technicalities and how Garrett had to be read his rights before they could talk. Then she purposefully misread the Miranda warnings. By the time she ran through them a second time—necessary to ensure proper procedure—she had Paul and Garrett convinced she was no threat to them. Both men visibly relaxed as Laney retook her seat.

"Now, let's talk about Mitch Caldwell." She bit the cap off her pen. "And don't hold back. Any detail could be important."

Garrett took a swig of his drink. "Mitch worked for me, off and on, for about three years. He was good with maps, and enjoyed camping, but... there was always something off about him. Especially when it came to women. He had a hard time understanding boundaries. I talked to him a few times, and he seemed to get better." He shrugged. "Guess he forgot everything I taught him when he moved to Mississippi."

A chill crept down Jonah's spine. Mitch had been arrested for stalking in Mississippi. This time he couldn't keep quiet. "Sounds like you were mentoring Mitch?"

"Mentoring is too strong of a word. Mitch had no game. He didn't know how to interact with women." His lips formed an arrogant smile. "I never had that issue, so I tried to help him."

"Did he have a temper?" Laney asked.

"A pretty volatile one. That was another issue I tried to help him with."

"Did you know he was back in town?"

Garrett nodded. "I saw him about two weeks ago, fishing on the lake. He had a broken pole and looked like he'd been camping out in the woods. He asked if I had any work for him, but I lied and said no. With his record, there was no way I could let him be around any customers. I haven't seen him since."

Laney pulled out a map of Piney Woods from her folder and set it on the table. "If Mitch wanted to hide out in the park, do you know where he would camp?"

He leaned over the map and studied it for a moment. He pointed to the area where Jonah and Laney had found evidence of an illegal campsite. "This is a good spot for that. Remote and not patrolled often by the rangers." After Laney circled it with a red pen, he tapped on another spot on the map. "Or this one. This is out where I saw Mitch fishing a few weeks ago."

Laney circled that one as well, tossing a discreet glance over her shoulder at Jonah. It wasn't a guarantee they'd find Mitch in that spot, but it was worth searching. Then she smiled at Garrett. "That's very helpful. Thank you." She returned the map to her file folder. "Do you have a boat, Garrett? Or access to one?"

The attorney placed a restraining hand on his client's arm. "Don't answer that." Paul turned his beady eyes on Laney. "My client has cooperated and told you what he knows about Mitch. Any other questions are out of bounds."

"Garrett and Mitch worked together for years, by his own admission. The man who committed these murders also used a boat in order to gain access to my cabin and shoot at me. After spending six years in prison for rape and stalking, I doubt Mitch has the cash to purchase a boat. It's more likely he stole it, and I'd like to know if it was Garrett's he took."

"It's all right, Paul." Garrett shook off his lawyer's restraining hand. "I want to help." He fixed his attention on Laney and nodded solemnly. "Yes, I have a small fishing dinghy that is stored on the lake in a cove. I've had it for years, and Mitch knows about it."

Jonah read between the lines. Garrett was keeping the boat illegally in the cove. But had he taken it out this morning, or had Mitch? He stepped forward. "Where were you today?"

"Again, we're getting into areas—"

He slammed his hands down on the table. "Four people are dead, counselor. Two of them were Garrett's friends. Supposedly." He shifted his glare toward Garrett. "Don't you want to help us capture the killer who murdered your friends? Or are you so heartless you don't care?"

"Of course I care!" Garrett's own temper flared as his cheeks heated.

Laney laid a hand on Jonah's arm. Her touch was so familiar, and yet never failed to grab his attention. "Please, Jonah. Back off. Your accusations are unwarranted."

He jerked away from her to prowl the room, and Laney offered an apologetic smile to Garrett and Paul. "I'm so sorry. He's very protective, and this morning was rattling for us both." She turned toward Garrett. "It would help a lot if you could confirm your whereabouts this morning, as well as for the times of the murders."

"My client has already informed you he was home alone during both murders." Paul sniffed.

"Of course. I forgot." Laney tapped her head as if she was dense. "And this morning?"

His lawyer attempted to prevent him from answering, but Garrett waved away the advice. "I was hiking in the woods near Bear Creek. This entire thing..." He swallowed hard. "Nolan and Lisa's murders... they were a shock. I haven't processed it all yet and needed some time to be alone and grieve."

"That's understandable." Laney tilted her head. "Bear Creek is pretty close to the second location you pointed out that Mitch could be using as a hideaway. Did you see him out that way?"

"No." Garrett's gaze narrowed, as if he was realizing that maybe Laney wasn't on his side after all. "Like I said, the last time I saw Mitch was two weeks ago."

"And now, I must insist we bring this interview to an end," Paul interjected. "My client is tired and grief-stricken."

Jonah nearly snorted at that. Garrett didn't look the least bit grief-stricken. But as the two men rose, Laney extended her hand toward Garrett. "Thank you so much for your help today. And I'm very sorry for your loss."

"Thank you." Garrett stared at her for a long moment, his giant hand holding her small, and more delicate one, for several seconds longer than was polite.

Jonah mashed his teeth together to keep from crossing the room and tearing Garrett's hand away from Laney's. His dislike of the man was visceral and immediate. He'd dealt with plenty of arrogant, boundary-crossing men in his career, but something about the way Garrett looked at Laney—like she was property to be claimed—made his blood boil.

Garrett and his attorney left the room. Jonah joined Laney in the hall to watch them cross the bullpen and exit into the parking lot.

"What do you think?" she asked.

"Garrett fits the profile. He knew Nolan and Lisa, and harassed Ava. He doesn't have an alibi for any of the attacks. He's definitely fascinated by you, and he has a boat. It all fits."

"Almost too perfectly," she murmured. "And how does Mitch fit into all of this?"

"He could be illegally camping in the park, hiding out from the police, and have nothing to do with the murders."

"True."

They were standing in a crowded sheriff's department, so taking her hand or embracing her would have been inappropriate. Still, Jonah needed to touch her. He extended his pinky, brushing against the soft curve of her palm. "You were amazing."

"*We* were amazing." Her lips quirked. "You snarled and gnashed your teeth so well I worried you might break a molar during the interview."

"I didn't like Garrett being near you," he confessed,

his voice barely above a whisper. "I almost tore his hand off his body when he wouldn't let go of you there at the end."

"Good thing you didn't," Laney replied, but then she turned her head and her breath hitched as their gazes met. Their pinkies were now twisted together, the touch so minor, and yet... Jonah felt it right down to his bones. And when Laney's gaze dropped to his mouth, it took serious restraint to stop himself from leaning forward and brushing a kiss on her gorgeous lips.

He had to hold steady. Be patient. Have faith.

It wasn't easy. The signals she was giving out were mixed, and at some point, they needed to address it. But Jonah would give her the space and time to sort through things.

She was worth it.

The door to the viewing room opened, and Chief Deputy Williams stormed out, quickly followed by Tate and Ryker. All of them wore grim and worried expressions.

Jonah's muscles tightened. "What is it?"

The chief deputy came to a stop in front of them. "I just got a call from dispatch." Her gaze shifted to Laney. "There's been an incident at your sister's house."

TWENTY-TWO

Laney's heart was in her throat as Jonah sped through the center of town. Her hands shook so badly, she couldn't have considered driving. She balled them into fists so tight her fingers hurt. Scout whimpered from her crate in the back, picking up on Laney's clear distress, and she made a calming shushing sound to reassure her dog. Chief Deputy Williams didn't have much information about the 911 call. Only that someone had been attacked and they needed an ambulance.

She knew she should pray but couldn't find the words.

Her sister was all the family she had... if she lost Bre...

Trembles racked her body.

"Hang in there, Laney." Jonah reached across the space separating them and placed a hand over her closed fist.

"She has to be okay." Tears pricked the back of her eyes, but she fought them back. Papa Earl. And baby

Asher. She didn't even know whether Marcus was at home tonight or at work. All of them could be hurt. Or worse. Laney almost never allowed herself to envision the worst, but right now, in this moment, she couldn't stop herself.

"God, we come to you with humble hearts." Jonah's voice was soft and reverent. "We ask that You watch over Breanna, Marcus, Asher, and Papa Earl. Give us the strength to face what comes next. Shine Your light on us so we may walk toward You even when things feel hopeless or dark. Amen."

"Amen," she whispered, feeling some of the tension coiling inside her belly loosen. She'd never been more grateful for her best friend. "Thank you, Jonah."

Moments later, they turned into her sister's neighborhood. Breanna's house was at the end of a cul-de-sac. Red and blue flashing lights from the responding patrol shimmered off the trees and yard. Laney hopped out of the SUV and raced across the grass. Papa Earl, his face half-obscured by an oxygen mask, was being loaded into the back of the ambulance. Breanna stood barefoot on the walkway in her pajamas, a stricken look on her face.

"Bre!" Laney hurried toward her sister and embraced her in a tight hug. "What happened?"

"Someone broke in and attacked Papa Earl." Bre swiped at the tears on her cheeks.

The EMT leaned out of the ambulance. "Are you riding with him, ma'am?"

"No, I have to stay here with the baby. My husband, Marcus Sullivan, is a nurse in the emergency room. He'll meet you when you get there." Breanna pulled out her phone and texted Marcus as the ambulance drove off.

Jonah and Scout joined them on the walkway. Laney quickly filled Jonah in on what Breanna had shared with her. The front door to the house hung wide open, but from Laney's vantage point, it didn't appear to have been busted down. She turned back to her sister. "Can you tell me exactly what happened?"

"I was putting Asher to sleep when there was a thump from the living room. I was worried Papa Earl had stumbled or fallen, so I went to check on him." Fresh tears filled her eyes. "He was lying in the foyer, uncon- scious, and the front door was hanging open. I caught a glimpse of someone wearing black running across the yard. He got into a vehicle and drove away." She looked bewildered. "Who would hurt a helpless elderly man?"

Laney felt a burst of anger flare inside her. "Did you catch the make and model of the vehicle the perpetrator escaped in?"

"It looked like a Jeep Cherokee. Black or dark blue."

The anger cemented into an icy rage. Laney met Jonah's gaze before wrapping an arm around her sister and shepherding her inside. "Did you hear the doorbell ring? Or a knock?"

"No, but I was nursing Asher and his white noise sound was on, plus my bedroom and the nursery are in the back of the house. I would've heard the doorbell, but its possible someone knocked and I missed it."

They bypassed some deputies and went into the kitchen. Laney pushed her sister into the closest chair and began making tea. The sound of crying came from the baby monitor. Breanna rushed from the room to check on Asher.

Jonah lingered in the doorway, speaking to a deputy. Chief Deputy Williams arrived. They all conferred quietly and then examined the doorframe. At some point, the chief deputy and her subordinate stepped outside with Jonah.

After a little, he joined Laney in the kitchen. "No sign of forced entry. Looks like Papa Earl must've heard a knock and answered the door. Then he was attacked." His expression was grim. "This has to be connected to the murders. Garrett couldn't have done it. He was sitting in an interview room down at the sheriff's department—"

"But Mitch could have." The water in the kettle began boiling, and she poured it into a cup. "We need to check the other area of the park Garrett showed us on the map. The one close to Bear Creek."

"Not tonight. It's too dangerous."

He was right. Even with numerous law enforcement personnel, it would be risky to traipse through the woods after a potential killer. Plus, there was the threat of more thunderstorms closing in. The Labor Day weekend had turned into a wet one. She wondered how many of the campers had abandoned their reservations or checked out early. With a killer on the loose, Laney was tempted to close the entire park down. She said as much to Jonah.

"It's worth thinking about. Rain will be on and off all week though. Considering the weather, I don't think you'll have that many people hiking or camping out." He placed a hand on her back, between her shoulder blades. "You've got rangers on patrol throughout the night, plus Tate and Ryker will stay at a cabin at the park. So far, the killer seems focused on you. I'm more worried about that."

"He isn't focused enough on me." That she could handle. But this... "He's gone after my family. After you." The rage churning in her stomach heated her from the inside out. "What game is he playing? If he wants me, then just come after me."

"No one's getting close to you. I won't allow it." His mouth quirked. "Neither will Scout. She's practically glued to your leg at the moment."

Despite the seriousness of the situation, Laney laughed. She reached down to stroke Scout's soft ears, and then, seeking comfort, closed the gap between her and Jonah, wrapping her arms around his waist. He immediately embraced her. The scent of peppermint soothed her raw nerves. His shirt was soft against her cheek, and the sound of his heart beat against her ear. Strong. Steady. Just like the man.

The thought of losing him... she couldn't bear it. She just couldn't. "I'm scared."

He let out a long and low sigh. "Me too, sweetheart."

The vulnerability in his voice made her heart ache. It also made her feel less lonely. Less lost. Laney lifted her head until she could look him in the eye. The warmth she found there was familiar, and yet... more intense. She realized with a jolt that Jonah had always held back. He'd been careful with his touches, cautious with his words, and guarded when he looked at her. Constantly afraid to show her the truth. Worried about how she might react.

And she realized then, in that moment, what it must've cost him. All those years of hiding his true feelings.

She didn't want him to hide. And she didn't want to hide anymore either.

So before the fear could take hold, Laney rose and kissed him.

His lips were warm and firm against hers. She tasted peppermint on his breath, felt the gentle pressure of his hands cupping her face as if she were something precious. Her pulse raced. As if of their own accord, her fingers traced a path up his chest and to the base of his neck where they buried themselves in the soft strands of his hair.

Jonah deepened the kiss, and she was lost. It was like coming home and stepping into the unknown all at once. Precious as a sunbeam, as fragile as a petal. The feeling was all-encompassing. And when Jonah finally pulled back, they were both breathless.

Jonah ran his thumb over the curve of her bottom lip. It tingled from his kiss. "Not that I'm complaining, but... why did you do that?"

"I..." She wasn't sure how to answer that. Her heart pounded against her rib cage, the pulse picking up as the fear settled in. "I didn't think about it beforehand. It... was..."

"That's what I thought." He dropped his hands from

her face and stepped back, leaning his large body against the counter. "I care about you, Laney. Truth be told, I'm in love with you and have been for a long time. I know what I want." His gaze lifted to meet hers. "I want a life with you. Forever."

Two warring battles raged inside her. One longed to step back into his embrace and kiss him again. The other was sheer panic at hearing the words *love* and *forever* together in one declaration. Unable to give in to either desire, her feet stayed rooted to the spot.

Jonah sighed. "I know what I'm saying scares you, sweetheart, but I'm not going anywhere. I'm here. Waiting." He brushed a strand of hair off her forehead. "Figure out what you want. Take the time you need to do it. All I ask is one thing. Don't kiss me again until you're certain. My heart can't take it."

Her chin trembled. A tornado of emotions whipped through her, stealing her breath and her ability to speak.

Jonah dropped his hand. "I'm going outside to confer with Chief Deputy Williams. She was going to check with the neighbors, see if anyone has a front door camera. We might uncover video of Papa Earl's attacker."

Laney nodded. A moment later, the front door closed.

The silence left behind was deafening.

TWENTY-THREE

Drizzle dampened Jonah's face and hair as he stepped off the small front porch onto the walkway. He'd forgotten his hat in the SUV earlier. One of the patrol cars was gone, but two others still sat at the curb. Chief Deputy Williams was speaking on the phone. She nodded in his direction and held up a finger, indicating he should wait.

Hopefully, she had good news.

Jonah retrieved his cowboy hat from Laney's SUV, settling it on his head, before tugging on a lightweight rain jacket. The glow from the kitchen window caught his attention. He watched for a moment but didn't see Laney. His pulse still hadn't settled from their kiss.

Had it been a mistake to tell her that he was in love with her? Jonah wasn't sure. All he knew was that his heart demanded he speak the truth. And after that kiss... well, if there had been any doubts about his feelings, they'd been erased completely. He loved her. Wanted to marry her. Have kids with her. A white-picket fence and a mortgage and arguments over where to spend the holidays. He wanted to wake up next to her and hold her in his arms as he fell asleep.

He wanted it all.

And buried underneath all of those desires was a bone-deep fear that Laney would reject him. That she'd conclude he wasn't enough for her. Because after that kiss, he'd seen those walls of hers shooting straight back up.

Hold steady. Have faith. Be patient.

Ryker's advice rang in his mind. Jonah breathed out and bowed his head. "Lord, I don't know what the future you have planned for me is, but my heart says Laney is in it. I want her in it. But I've done all I can to show her that we belong together. So I lift up this problem to You."

Considering the danger they faced, and Papa Earl's unknown condition, it seemed selfish to pray for his relationship with Laney. But Jonah knew how to solve cases. And he trusted the doctors to do all they could for Papa Earl. In those things, he knew the path forward. His relationship with Laney however... that was a gray area that triggered all of his deepest insecurities.

The subsequent peace that washed over him following the prayer centered his emotions. Inexplicably, the burden on his shoulders felt lighter, as if he'd done all he could about his feelings for Laney.

Raising his head, he noticed Chief Deputy Williams finishing up her call. He approached. "Any news?"

"Next-door neighbor has a front doorbell camera.

Caught the assailant." She tapped on the phone screen, pulling up a video.

The footage was grainy, but Jonah could identify Mitchell Caldwell as he stealthily approached the house. A few minutes passed, and then Mitch appeared again, this time running across the grass. He hopped into a black Jeep Cherokee parked across the street and took off.

Jonah stiffened. He'd suspected Mitch was behind the assault, but seeing him on the security footage cemented his suspicions into hard evidence. "I'll need a copy of this video."

She nodded. "I've already alerted Ryker and Tate to be on the lookout. Laney should advise her rangers as well. Chances are, this mole we're hunting is going back into hiding somewhere on the park grounds." The chief deputy frowned. "He took a big risk by attacking Papa Earl. What message is he hoping to send? That he can get to Laney's family?"

"Maybe." Something about the entire situation didn't sit right with Jonah, but he couldn't put his finger on what it was. "When we interviewed Garrett, I was certain he was the killer."

"Me too."

"Could they be working together?" He mused aloud. "It's uncommon among killers, but it's not unheard of. Emilia Knox was involved in a serial killer case in which there were two perpetrators working together... Hold on. Let me call her." He dialed Emilia's number and put her on speaker. Quickly, he explained the evidence they had against Mitch and asked about his theory.

Emilia was quiet for a long moment. "There's no evidence there was more than one assailant in the cabin. And Laney was attacked by only one person. So I think we're dealing with a single killer. But... it's possible our killer and Mitch crossed paths. Mitch is desperate, in need of cash, and hiding out in the woods. He could be manipulated or blackmailed into working for the killer."

"Working how?" Chief Deputy Williams asked.

"By keeping tabs on Laney," Jonah filled in. "Think about it. Mitch was fishing in an area of the park that was marked as forbidden. When Laney confronted him, he bolted like a scared rabbit. That's not the action of someone bold enough to march into a cabin or a campsite and murder two people. Mitch was there because Garrett couldn't be."

His gaze shot to Breanna's house. "Garrett was escorted down to the sheriff's department. He requested his attorney, knew he'd be there for hours. Since he came in willingly and wasn't under arrest, he would've still had his cell phone. He could've contacted Mitch at any time. It would explain why Papa Earl was attacked." He turned back to the chief deputy. "He's setting up Mitch to take the fall for everything."

Emilia's voice spilled from the phone speaker. "That could be the killer's plan, and it would fit with what we know. The real problem is that if Garrett is our killer, he knows Mitch is on law enforcement's radar and he's going to get desperate. Garrett will need to act fast to complete his mission and kill Mitch before anyone is any the wiser." She paused. "Jonah, he's obsessed with Laney. It was obvious in the interview."

"He's going to make a play for her."

"And you. The killer has an MO. Kill the significant other in front of the female victim and then attack her. He won't want Laney on her own. He needs you both."

Jonah's muscles tightened. "We need to find Garrett. Now."

Laney set a fresh cup of tea on the small table next to her sister's rocking chair. Breanna was holding Asher, slowly swaying him back to sleep. She smiled her thanks. "I heard from Marcus." She kept her voice at a whisper to avoid waking the baby. "Papa Earl is awake and as ornery as ever. He suffered a slight bump to the head, and they want to keep him overnight, but it looks like he's going to be just fine."

"Praise God." Laney breathed out a sigh of relief. She tucked herself into the corner of the couch with her own cup of tea. Jonah was still outside with Chief Deputy Williams. Laney should join them, but after everything that'd happened tonight, she wanted just a few minutes of normal. Or maybe she just wanted to be with her sister.

The soft glow from the lantern on the side table illuminated the paint cans in the corner. She tilted her chin toward them. "You decided on Mindful Gray. Good choice."

Bre nodded. "You were right. It'll bring out the yellow in the wood floors." She was quiet for a beat. "So... when were you going to tell me that you and Jonah were dating?"

Laney nearly choked on her tea. She sputtered and used a napkin to wipe her mouth. "We're not."

Breanna leveled a look in her direction. "I saw the two of you kissing in the kitchen."

"Oh." She blushed and squirmed on the couch. "Well... that wasn't what it looked like."

"It looked like two people in love." Breanna's mouth stretched into a giant grin. "And it's long overdue. The two of you have been dancing around each other for more than a decade. It's about time you both realized what the rest of us already knew."

Her brain short-circuited. "The... rest of us?"

"Me. Marcus. Papa Earl. Ryker. Tate. My neighbor across the street. Basically, anyone with eyeballs."

She groaned and laid her head back on the couch, hiding her face in her hands. "You're making that up."

"Umm, no, I'm not." Breanna tilted her head, her dark hair falling over one shoulder. "What's the matter, sis? There's no reason to keep it a secret. Everyone will be overjoyed. We love you, and we love Jonah. Seeing the two of you together and happy is the best thing ever."

Laney dropped her hands. "Because... I'm not sure we're going to be together. It's... complicated."

Breanna stopped rocking. "What are you talking about?" Her vision narrowed. "Please do not tell me you are letting your fear of commitment get in the way of this?"

"I don't have a fear of commitment."

She gave a very unladylike snort. "You're so scared of commitment, you've practically got one foot out the door at all times. You never settle down anywhere, always moving every few years. You change boyfriends like I change socks."

"Ew. First of all, change your socks more often. Like every day."

Breanna waved off the comment. "You know what I mean." Her expression grew sad, and her voice soft. "I know you're itching to move again. I can feel it, and I've been holding my breath waiting for you to tell me that you're going."

Guilt swamped Laney. "I'm sorry, Bre. I don't mean to hurt you. And I don't want to hurt Jonah." She bit her lip. "This is who I am. I think it's who I'll always be."

"No, Laney. It's who you *choose* to be." Her sister let that comment hang heavy in the air, and then said, "If you were happy, I wouldn't think twice about it, but I know you're not. You're scared. And you're running. The real question is why?"

Tears pricked her eyes. She was exhausted, her emotions raw. The attacks, the pending job offer, these feelings for Jonah... it was all bearing down on her. Normally, Laney would run. But now, she didn't have the strength to fight against it anymore. "Jonah says he's in love with me. And I believe him. But you and I both know that love doesn't last forever. People change." She swiped at the runaway tear on her cheek. "Dad did."

Breanna's expression softened. "And you're afraid that Jonah will become like Dad?"

"Not exactly like Dad. But maybe one day, Jonah will wake up and realize that he's not in love with me anymore. It happens. And if I give my heart to him..." Laney choked up. "I'm too much like Mom. I can't go back. If I give my heart to him, and he walks away, I'll never recover. I can't do it, Bre. I just... can't."

She dissolved into tears. Her sister rose from the rocking chair and left the room. When she came back, she didn't have Asher anymore. Instead, she carried a box of tissues.

She sat next to Laney on the sofa and handed her a few. "I have a confession to make. You're not going to like that I kept it a secret, but I think you need to hear it."

Laney mopped her face and sniffed. "What is it?"

"I met with Dad."

Shock vibrated through her. "You what?" She blinked to clear her vision from the tears. "When?"

"After Mom passed. All I knew about him was the little you and Mom had told me. I wanted to meet him and see for myself what kind of person he was." She rested a hand on Laney's knee. "And you know what I discovered? Dad was on his fourth marriage. He spent the entire time we were together talking about himself. Never once did he ask about Marcus or Asher. Or even you."

"What are you saying?"

"Dad was always a selfish person, sis. I know you remember him as a loving father. I'm glad that you do, but I think your perception is skewed because you were so young when he left." Breanna let her process that for a minute and then continued, "Mom fell in love with the wrong kind of man. I'm sure she thought he would change. And after it fell apart, she couldn't let go. But what she held on to... I don't think it ever existed in the first place."

Laney swallowed hard. Could Breanna be right? It was hard to know. "We can't be certain of that."

"You're right. We can't. But there is something you can be certain of." She lightly touched Laney's chest. "Your own heart. God wants you to be happy, Laney. He is a loving and kind Father who only wants the best for you. If you look inside your heart, and find that Jonah is there, then trust in that. Don't let what happened between Mom and Dad rob you of the happiness that is meant for you."

Fresh tears swelled. Her sister's words hit home, and Laney desperately wanted to believe... "I'm scared, Bre. What if I can't do it?"

"You are the smartest and bravest person I've ever met. No one loves more strongly or is more dedicated than you. Except for maybe... Jonah." Breanna smiled. "He's a good man. He's stood by your side for the last fifteen years, through difficult times. If anyone has proven themselves, it's him. Take the leap of faith, Laney."

She bristled at her sister's commanding tone. "How do you know that's what's in my heart?"

"Because I've seen the two of you together. That kind of love can't be faked." Breanna's expression was understanding but firm. "Ultimately, the decision is yours. God—and I—can only do so much."

Laney grabbed a pillow and smacked her sister with it, laughing. "I hate when you talk down to me."

"Then don't be short-sighted and I won't have to." Breanna smacked Laney with a much larger pillow.

The two of them continued whacking each other childishly until they were both on the floor in a puddle of giggles. Laney couldn't stop laughing. Her cheeks hurt from it.

She hugged her sister. "I love you."

"Love you too. Now help me pick these pillows up off the floor."

That set off a fresh round of giggles. It was a side effect of the stress, and a relief that they were all safe. But as Laney put the last pillow onto the couch, her cell phone rang. She glanced at the screen. It was one of her night rangers on patrol. Concern immediately shot through her as she answered the call. "What's wrong?"

"We have a missing child."

TWENTY-FOUR

Laney gripped the steering wheel of her vehicle as she flew down the highway toward Piney Woods. It was only nine o'clock, but it felt like the day would never end. A shooting, questioning Garrett, the attack on Papa Earl, and now a missing child. It felt like she hadn't had a minute to catch her breath.

"So you think Garrett and Mitch are working together?" She spared a glance at Jonah.

He held onto the handle above the door with one strong hand. The streetlights played across the curve of his nose and his high forehead before casting them back into shadows. He hadn't shaved since early this morning, and bristles covered his cheeks and chin. She knew intimately what they'd felt like as he'd kissed her, and she tore her gaze away to focus on the road.

The conversation with Breanna weighed heavily in her mind. Laney was half-tempted to blurt out everything. Her fears. Her feelings. She realized now how silly it was to have kept them to herself. Jonah had been right that day in the woods. They were friends first. Best friends. And they always found a way through difficult things together. If she'd told him what was going on in her head and her heart...

Then maybe they wouldn't be in this mess now.

Because she loved him. She knew that with every fiber of her being. It didn't erase the fears, or her worries, but... Breanna had been right. Jonah was in her heart. He'd been there for a very long time, and together, with prayer and patience, maybe they could find a way forward.

But this was not the time to go into all of that. Not with a killer on the loose and a missing child to find.

"We can't be certain Garrett and Mitch are working together, but it makes sense." Jonah looked down at his phone. "Chief Deputy Williams says that Garrett isn't at home. They've contacted his lawyer, but if he knows where Garrett is, he's not saying."

Laney turned through the main gate of the park and raced for the visitor center. She hopped out of her SUV, released Scout, and then hurried up the walkway. They were met by Ranger Zoe Papadopoulos, whose worried expression and clipped tone immediately conveyed the child hadn't been found yet. "The family is staying in Cabin 10. According to the parents, they were roasting marshmallows with another family and their kids when their four-year-old disappeared."

"How long has she been missing?"

"Approximately an hour. The parents spent some

time looking for her on their own before calling the park's emergency line. Chief Ranger Dawson was working late, so he responded along with me. He's currently at the campsite, as are Ryker and Tate. They're searching the area and talking to nearby campers." Zoe lifted a plastic evidence bag. "I collected a blanket from the child's bed for Scout."

A grateful surge washed through Laney. Zoe had followed perfect protocol by collecting a scent item before anyone had even suggested it. Despite the chaos of recent days, her rangers were performing exactly as trained.

"Thank you." She took the blanket, her heart aching at the sight of the pink fabric covered in cartoon princesses. "Where are the parents?"

"Inside the lobby."

"And the girl's name?"

"Alli Yates. Her parents are Sarah and Harry Yates."

Laney's entire body stiffened. "Alli Yates. Red-hair, blue eyes, 3 feet 2 inches, and around 35 pounds?" When Zoe nodded, Laney's stomach dropped. She turned to Jonah. "It's the same little girl I helped the other day, the one who fell down."

The worry and anger roiling through her were reflected in his expression. "That can't be a coincidence."

She didn't think so either, but they needed to be strategic. "We can't jump to conclusions. Alli may have wandered away. She's done it before. While I speak to the parents, call Ryker. Get an update on their search."

He nodded and moved off while she headed inside to

speak to Alli's parents. Both of them were distraught. Sarah's eyes were swollen from crying, and her husband looked lost. Laney introduced herself.

Sarah's eyes widened. "You helped Alli when she got hurt." Her gaze dropped to Scout. "Alli's been talking nonstop about your dog..." She dissolved into tears again, pressing her face into her husband's shoulder.

He kept an arm around her. "Alli's independent, and she's wandered off before, but never too far. We searched all the campsites near us... called her name..." He seemed bewildered. "She was right there. Playing with the other kids. And then the next..."

"We're doing everything we can to find her. I have my staff and the Texas Rangers on site. The Kirkland County Sheriff's Department is en route." Laney knew her attempt at comfort fell on deaf ears. These parents would not be whole until their child was back in their arms. "Does Alli have any medical conditions?"

"She has asthma." Harry pulled an inhaler out of his jacket pocket. "It can be severe, especially if she gets upset or exerts herself too much."

The worry in his expression cut Laney to the core. It also amplified the urgency in finding Alli. If she had been kidnapped, the stress of the event could trigger an asthma attack. Even if Alli had wandered away on her own, the fear of finding herself in the woods at night could be deadly.

Laney extended her hand. "May I take that with me?"

"Of course."

"Do you have any other inhalers? At the campsite maybe?"

Sarah wiped her face with a crumpled tissue. "There's one in Alli's backpack. And another inside my purse on the counter in the small kitchen."

"Okay. My ranger, Zoe, will stay here with you. She'll be in constant contact with the search teams and provide continuous updates."

Harry rose. "I should come with you—"

"No, sir." The last thing Laney wanted either of these parents was to discover the worst had happened on scene. She prayed Alli would be found alive and unharmed, but as much as her heart longed for that, she needed to follow protocol. "The best thing you can do to help us is to stay here. We may have questions that only you can answer, and we need to be able to reach you quickly."

Laney spared a few more precious moments reassuring the parents and then conferred with Zoe, ensuring she would stay at the visitor center and help coordinate. Before leaving, Laney grabbed a walkie-talkie in order to communicate with her team. Then she stepped back outside onto the sidewalk, Scout at her side.

Jonah hung up the phone and turned to face her. "Alli's still missing. Ryker says there aren't any witnesses, but someone in a neighboring campsite saw a black Jeep Cherokee speeding down the main road around the time of the disappearance."

Her worst fears were coming to fruition. "If Alli was taken by car, then Scout won't be able to track her. We need to find the Jeep and use that as a starting point. Call

Ryker back. Tell him and Tate to head toward Bear Creek ASAP, toward the area Garrett told us about in his interview."

She jogged to her vehicle, and a minute later, was racing down the main road of the park. While Jonah spoke with his colleagues, Laney used the radio to communicate with Andy. She informed him that Alli was an asthmatic and where the additional inhalers were. "Ryker says that a black Jeep Cherokee was spotted leaving the area around the time of the kidnapping. Expand your search to look for it." She rattled off the license plate number. "It's the same Cherokee registered to Nolan Carlson."

"The murder victim?"

"Yes, we think the killer stole his vehicle and is using it to get around. It's also a strong possibility Alli has been kidnapped. The primary suspect is Mitch Caldwell. The secondary suspect is Garrett Wheeler. If you see either man, consider them armed and dangerous. Act accordingly."

"Understood. Are you coming to Campsite 10?"

"No. I have a potential lead on the Jeep that I want to check out. I'll be in touch if we find anything." She signed off and dropped the radio into the cupholder.

Jonah grabbed the handle as she deviated from the main road onto a smaller one. "Garrett could've been lying about where Mitch likes to hide out. It's not guaranteed we'll find the Jeep there."

"I know, but it's the only lead we have at the moment."

Her cell phone rang, the name flashing across her dashboard. Brett Harrison. He'd likely heard about the kidnapping and was calling to offer to help. Laney normally appreciated his get-to-it attitude, but it was times like this that his need to impress her was a challenge. Instead of calling her, Brett should be following protocol and phoning the staff line, which Zoe would manage.

She nearly let the call go to voicemail, but a whispered instinct told her to answer it. "Superintendent Torres."

"Hey, boss," Brett's words were whispered. "I found Mitch Caldwell."

Her heart stuttered, and she let up on the gas. "What?"

"I spotted him driving a Jeep through the park and followed it. I was careful… hung back so he wouldn't see me, you know. The Jeep is here on a dirt road near Bear Creek. I've parked my truck down a ways and am heading through the woods on foot—"

"Don't take another step!" Laney commanded, her tone sharp and unyielding. "Mitch Caldwell is a wanted criminal. He's possibly armed and dangerous. Head back to your truck immediately. I'm on my way. Send me a pin so I know your exact coordinates."

"You got it, boss."

He hung up, and a second later there was a text message with his coordinates. Laney braked completely and navigated to the location. "This is on the outer edge of the park boundaries. There's a well-used hiking trail that overlooks the limestone bluff and the creek, but not much else. It's the perfect place for Mitch to be hiding out."

"How close is this location to the area Garrett indicated on the map?"

"It's near, but it's not the same." She forwarded the pinned location to Jonah, as well as the other Texas Rangers. Scout whimpered from the back seat, picking up on the tension. She glanced behind her. "It's okay, girl." But there was worry buried in her dog's eyes. Was she concerned about Laney? Or had hearing Brett's voice over the car's speakers upset her?

Laney inhaled sharply as an idea jabbed her. "Oh... Jonah. What if we've been wrong this entire time? What if the killer is someone who wasn't on our suspect list at all?"

His head swiveled to face her. "What are you talking about?"

"Brett." Her mind raced. "As the front desk clerk, he interacts with everyone on staff, including the volunteers. Everyone goes through the visitor center. He checked in Ava and Tyler, along with Lisa and Nolan. His cologne smells the same as the killer's. Scout nearly bit him when he got too close to me. He was in the lobby on the day Alli got hurt... and now he just happens to spot Mitch driving through the park at the same moment we're searching for Alli..."

She'd never quite bought Garrett's involvement in the murders. It made logical sense, but there had always been a niggling doubt she couldn't quite dislodge. "Brett knows Garrett. They're buddies. He may even know where Garrett's boat is kept and what the combination code to the lock is."

Horror sank into her as she realized too late what she should have known all along. "Brett could be the killer."

TWENTY-FIVE

Darkness pressed against Jonah, the pitch-black woods alive with prey and predators.

He pulled a bulletproof vest from the back of Ryker's SUV and carried it to Laney, who was shifting through a backpack of supplies. "Put this on." His own was already in place, and in one hand he carried a rifle. Night vision goggles would've proven helpful but weren't part of the standard equipment Texas Rangers carried. After this, he intended to add several sets to his vehicle.

Laney took the Kevlar and slipped it over her head. She attempted to attach the straps, but they were tangled. Jonah laid his rifle down in the back of her SUV and reached around her slender waist. He separated the straps, bringing them around and securing the Velcro. Touching her, even like this, sent a longing through him.

There was so much he wanted to say. Time wouldn't allow it. And so, once she had her vest on, he took her hands and bowed his head. "Lord, we ask that You watch over us and Alli. Help us bring this little girl to safety and give us the wisdom and strength to capture everyone responsible for these horrible crimes."

"Amen," Laney whispered.

Jonah raised his head, and their gazes met. He couldn't see her eyes clearly in the darkness, his vision only able to make out the contours of her face. Rising on her toes, she took him by surprise when her mouth brushed against his. The kiss was nothing more than a whisper. Petal soft and tender. Full of promise.

His heart pounded against his rib cage. "Laney…"

"No time, Foster." She jerked her chin toward something behind him. "Ryker, Tate, you guys ready?"

Jonah turned to find his teammates standing nearby. Like him and Laney, they'd suited up in bulletproof vests underneath lightweight rain jackets. Each carried a rifle and wore a backpack filled with supplies, like water, basic first aid, and protein bars.

"Let's do this," Ryker whispered. They'd parked on a side road hidden in the trees. The sheriff's department and the state police were sending additional reinforcements to their location, but it would take an hour for them to coordinate.

Alli may not have that much time. It was a serious risk they were taking, but each of them agreed it was worth it. Jonah had never been prouder to serve alongside such dedicated law enforcement officers. This was why he'd chosen this path, and what his family could never understand. Moments like these. When everything else fell away except the mission: protecting the innocent, pursuing justice, standing in the gap when no one else could.

Laney shrugged on her backpack before grabbing the evidence bag with Alli's blanket. Scout, already dressed in a SAR working dog vest, pranced in the dirt with excitement. She knew it was time to work.

"We need to get closer to the Jeep," Laney said. "Scout needs a starting point where Alli's scent might be present. The blanket will help her know what to look for, but we need to be in an area where Alli has been."

Jonah nodded. "We move together, tight formation. Mitch could be lying in wait, watching for us. Garrett may be working with him, and we still aren't certain about Brett's involvement. He could be friend or foe. Stay alert and vigilant."

He took the lead. Scout followed, then Laney, with Ryker and Tate bringing up the rear. Clouds covered the moon, and a soft drizzle began as they trekked through the woods. A nondescript truck came into view, parked on the dirt road. Laney grabbed Jonah's arm and whispered, "That's Brett's vehicle."

There were no signs of the man. Jonah eased beyond the shelter of the trees to look inside the cab. Empty. He touched the hood of the truck and found that it was still warm. He slipped back inside the shelter of the woods. "Let's keep moving."

Brett was either their killer, lost in the woods, or dead. Adrenaline and hyper-vigilance increased Jonah's heart rate. He took deep breaths to slow it down and prevent his vision from clouding at the edges. A short distance ahead, the Jeep Cherokee came into view. The license plate number, barely visible in the darkness, confirmed it was Nolan Carlson's. Stolen from his cabin on the night of his murder. The same vehicle Mitch had driven away in after attacking Papa Earl.

It was parked on their side of the dirt road. Laney wasted no time. She opened the evidence bag containing Alli's blanket and offered it to Scout. "Scent."

The lab stuck her nose in the blanket and took several deep breaths before Laney pulled it away. "Find."

Scout trotted a short distance away, lifting her nose in the air before sniffing various places on the ground. Laney held onto a retractable leash. She let out more of the lead as Scout continued to hunt for Alli's scent in the woods. Jonah held his breath. He'd seen the lab work several times, and knew she was amazing, but certain things could prevent her from picking up the smell. The recent rains, wind, certain terrain. If Mitch carried Alli or placed her in another vehicle—like an ATV—that could also interfere.

Suddenly, Scout's posture changed. Her tail lifted, and she started moving with purpose.

Laney took off after her dog, and Jonah increased his pace as well. His heart thundered against his rib cage. The perpetual drizzle was a constant background noise that made it hard to distinguish other sounds. He was terrified they were walking directly into a trap but didn't know how to stop it. Not with Alli's life at risk.

Scout led them to a small campsite. The tent was flimsy and big enough only for one person. The lab sniffed at the ground near the opening before abandoning it and moving on. Jonah gestured to Tate, who held his rifle at the ready to cover him. Then Jonah unzipped the tent's opening and pulled it back.

Empty. A sweep of the interior revealed a sleeping bag, a paperback book, and candy wrappers.

"I've got something." Ryker's voice was low but carried across the distance. He pointed to a tennis shoe on the other side of the camp. It was child-sized, pink with sparkles. "She's been here."

Scout was sniffing the borders of the woods. Laney led her to the shoe and ordered her to scent. She did and then shifted to that area of the campsite. Once again, her tail straightened, and she tugged at the leash with determination, plowing back into the trees.

They continued on for half a klick up steeper terrain before reaching the edge of a limestone bluff. The sound of Bear Creek rumbling and tumbling its way toward the lake became louder. Scout stopped near the wooden fence, put in place to prevent people from falling off the bluff, and whined.

Laney removed a small flashlight from her pocket and shone it over the edge. Her eyes widened. "She's here."

Jonah joined her at the fence. He caught sight of the little girl hanging from a branch several meters down. She was unconscious, and from this distance, it wasn't possible to tell if she was breathing. Jonah couldn't be sure how she'd even gotten there. Had she fallen? Been pushed?

"Here." Laney handed him the flashlight before stripping off her backpack. She ripped open the main pocket and dug around inside, unearthing a harness and rope. "I'll rappel down to retrieve her."

Jonah was tempted to argue with that plan. On the bluff, they were exposed. Ryker and Tate were standing guard, keeping watch, but the hair on the back of his neck rose anyway. He shone the beam down toward Alli. The rain had made the limestone slippery and treacherous. He could envision a thousand ways this could all go sideways quickly.

But he also couldn't figure out a better alternative.

He needed to trust Laney to do her job. And he needed to do his.

Protect her.

"What do you need me to do?" he asked.

She handed him the end of the rope and a locking carabiner. "Do you remember the knots I taught you?" After he gave a sharp nod, she gestured to a sturdy pine tree. "Secure the rope to that tree as close to the base as you can."

He slung his rifle over one shoulder and went to do her bidding as Laney removed her bulletproof vest before stepping into her harness. She checked her equipment with practiced efficiency. Her military training was evident in every precise movement.

"I'll need you to belay me," she said, pulling on a pair of tactical gloves before handing him the brake end of the rope.

"Got it."

"Keep it taut but give me enough slack to maneuver. If I call for more rope, feed it through slowly."

She moved to the edge, positioning herself with her back to the drop. Scout whined anxiously, trying to follow.

"Stay, Scout," Laney commanded.

The lab reluctantly obeyed, ears flattened with concern.

Jonah positioned himself in the belaying stance, wrapping the line around his body in the proper configuration. Their eyes met briefly, and a world of unspoken emotion passed between them.

"Be careful," he said.

"Always am."

She gave him a quick smile before leaning back into empty air, her weight transferring to the rope. Jonah felt the tension as she began her descent, feeding the rope through his hands with controlled precision. Laney walked her feet down the rock face, pushing off slightly to control her descent. The rain made the limestone dangerously slick, but she moved with confidence, testing each foothold before committing her weight.

"About five feet to your right," Jonah called down, keeping the flashlight trained on Alli's small form.

Laney adjusted her trajectory, working her way across the face of the bluff. She had to pause twice to clear the rope when it caught on jutting rock, each time hanging suspended by the harness while she worked the line free. When she reached Alli, she braced her feet against the rock and reached out, touching the child's neck. Even from above, Jonah could see her shoulders sag with relief.

"She's alive," Laney called up. "Pulse is weak but steady. She's caught in some branches, and her jacket is snagged. I need both hands free to work her loose."

"I've got you," he called back, locking the rope to hold Laney's position. His muscles flexed with the effort. The rain picked up from a drizzle to a light downpour. It soaked his hair and dripped down his face.

Carefully, using both hands, Laney examined Alli before lifting her into her arms. She secured her to the harness with another rope before lifting her face up to Jonah. "I'm going to keep going down. It'll be easier and safer than trying to make my way back up."

"Got it."

He continued to let out the line, and slowly Laney and Alli descended. He monitored their progress with the flashlight beam, his chest tight with every inch they moved. His muscles strained from the effort of holding the brake rope.

A sudden shout from Tate cut through the night.

Jonah whipped his head around.

A burst of gunfire came from the trees.

TWENTY-SIX

A sudden jerk of the rope sent Laney into momentary freefall.

Her stomach bottomed out, and the rock face loomed. Acting on instinct, she twisted to shield Alli with her body as they crashed into the bluff. Sharp pain shot through her forearm as the rough limestone sliced through her jacket and into her skin.

The sound of gunfire erupted above her. Multiple shots—not just one—from automatic rifles.

Terror gripped her heart. Jonah. He'd been exposed at the edge, holding her line. Had he been hit? Was he—

No. She couldn't let herself think that way. Not now.

Alli needed her to keep it together and get them off this bluff.

Laney assessed their position. The rope was now dangerously slack. Whatever was happening at the top, Jonah could no longer safely control her descent. Warm blood trickled down her arm from her wound. Alli's seemingly lifeless form rested against her, but the faint puff of her breath against Laney's neck reassured her that the child was still alive.

She glanced down. Maybe ten feet to the ground now. A risky fall, but survivable. Especially compared to the danger of hanging here while a gunfight raged above.

Making a split-second decision, she shifted Alli's weight, securing the child tightly against her with her injured arm. With her good hand, she reached for the quick-release mechanism on her harness. "Hold on, sweetheart," she whispered to the unconscious child. "This is going to be rough."

Laney took a deep breath, said a quick prayer, and hit the release.

For a moment, they were in freefall, the world reduced to wind and rain and the weight of Alli against her chest. She bent her knees to absorb the impact, rolling to her side as they hit the ground to protect Alli from the brunt of the fall.

Pain exploded through her ankle and hip as they tumbled onto the rocky shore. Laney landed on her back, the wind knocked out of her. Her chest felt like it would explode. Stars danced across her vision. She groaned and forced herself to roll to the side. Little Alli had stayed safe in her arms. Laney deposited the child onto the ground and focused on trying to deepen her breathing. Gradually, the pain in her chest faded.

The rain was relentless. It soaked Laney's hair and pelted her face. The sound of gunfire was still echoing above her. Her friends were in danger, and she was helpless to assist them. Every instinct screamed at her to find a way back up that bluff, to join the fight, to protect her team. But the unconscious child beside her changed everything.

Laney forced herself onto her knees, wincing as her injured ankle protested. She gently examined Alli, checking for broken bones or head trauma. The girl's breathing was shallow but steady. Her pulse was weak but regular. She was alive but needed medical attention soon. Laney reached for her radio but found only a shattered casing. It'd broken when she slammed into the limestone.

She pulled her cell phone from her pocket. The glow of the screen confirmed her worst fear. No cell service.

Laney glanced up at the bluff. The gunfire had become more sporadic.

God, please keep them safe. And help me protect this little girl.

Lifting Alli into her arms, she ignored the shooting pain in her hip and ankle as she stood. The hiking path along Bear Creek was several miles, nothing for her normally, but with her injured arm and leg, it would be slow going. Cognizant of the fact that there were unknown enemies in these woods, Laney pulled her service weapon from its holster. She limped forward.

The trail was muddy. The creek rumbled past, swollen from the recent storms. Pain vibrated through her with every step, but Laney tuned it out. Mind over matter. Her military days had taught her that.

A twig snapped nearby. Her breath hitched as a man stepped out of the darkness into her path.

Laney raised her weapon. "Don't move, or I'll shoot you."

"Boss, it's me." Brett's hushed whisper crossed the distance between them as his hands jerked into the air.

She didn't lower her weapon. Fear gripped her. "Stay away from me."

Brett's breathing was rapid. "Please. You have to help me. Mitch has a gun. I got away, but heard the shooting and…" He stepped closer, and the whites of his eyes shone in terror. "I don't know how to get out of here."

Her grip on her weapon remained steady, but doubt crept in. What if she'd been wrong? What if Brett was a victim like them? Garrett could be the one working with Mitch. Or they could all be wrong and Mitch was working on his own.

Brett's fear looked genuine. He was trembling, and his breathing was rapid. The rain had plastered his hair to his forehead, making him look younger than his 28 years. Indecision warred within her. Alli's weight grew heavier in her arms, and pain throbbed through her injured ankle.

"You're hurt." Brett eased closer. "Let me help you. I'll carry the little girl, and you can show me the way back."

She hesitated. And then, Laney lowered her weapon slightly.

A gunshot rang out.

Blood bloomed on Brett's shirt. He collapsed.

Laney whirled around, but it was too late. A dark shadow rushed her. Arms wrapped around her waist and the assailant took her down like a professional linebacker. Her weapon flew from her hand and landed somewhere in the dark as she slammed into the unyielding ground. Her scalp was punctured by the sharp pebbles littering the path, sending pain shooting through her. She lay momentarily stunned.

It was the only opening the attacker needed. He shoved Alli away and climbed on top of Laney, trapping her arms next to her sides. His expression was triumphant as he leaned over her. "Gotcha."

Garrett Wheeler.

He stared down at her with the cold-eyed gaze of a monster. A killer.

"You." She wheezed. Her lungs burned for air. For the second time, they'd had the wind knocked out of them.

A wicked smile twisted his features. "Me." He leaned closer, his finger trailing the curve of her face. Smelling his cologne, that sickening spicy scent, coupled with his touch made her want to gag. He hadn't been wearing it during their first interview. Garrett, like many men, must have more than one cologne and changed them out. "Getting to you wasn't easy. It took a lot of thinking. But you and I are going to have a good time together. I promise."

His breath was hot and disgusting against her face. Laney shuddered inside but forced herself to meet his gaze. Men like Garrett fed on their victims' terror. She would not show him an ounce of fear. "Deputies know where we are," she bluffed. "And the Texas Rangers have captured your buddy Mitch and will be here before long."

"Oh, I don't think so." He leaned back, trailing his finger down her throat and along the collar of her uniform. "Mitch is a better shot than I am with a rifle. I missed Jonah at your cabin, but he won't fail. Those rangers are dead. Along with your stupid dog. The deputies, and the rest of the park rangers, only know the location of the Jeep. It'll take them quite some time to figure out where you went."

Her heart froze in fear. No. He had to be lying.

Jonah wasn't dead.

He couldn't be.

Tears pricked her eyes. He didn't know. Didn't know that she loved him. Why hadn't she said it at the car when she kissed him? Or before going over the bluff?

Or two days ago.

Or ten years ago.

She was a foolish, foolish woman. She'd been in love with Jonah since the moment she first saw him. There'd never been anyone else for her. She'd broken things off after a month of dating, but when Jonah suggested just being friends, she'd jumped at the chance. Even then, she knew. Knew she needed him in her life.

He'd broken down every one of her barriers. Wormed his way into her heart day-by-day. A friendly ear to tell her problems to, gift packages when they were apart, vacations taken together, long talks late at night.

Holding her hand at her mother's funeral. Her sister's wedding. Asher's birth.

Birthdays. Christmases. Attending church together.

There wasn't one major incident in her life in the last ten years Jonah hadn't been a part of. The good and the bad.

She loved him. And she'd allowed fear to hold her back. Fear of abandonment. Fear of the future. Fear of truly handing him her heart and trusting that he would keep it safe. Laney had thought nothing could be worse than loving Jonah and losing him. But there was worse.

It was losing Jonah without him ever knowing how much he meant to her.

"Did you hear the gunshots?" Garrett asked gleefully, pulling her back into the present. Into this living, breathing nightmare she was facing. "Normally I like to kill a woman's significant other in front of her, but you and Jonah proved to be a challenge."

Laney eased one of the hands trapped next to her body down to the ground. She clawed at the gravel and dirt. "You tried to shoot Jonah at my cabin. You put the rabbit on the porch for him."

"Good job. You figured it out."

Out of the corner of her eye, she could see Brett lying motionless. "Brett?"

"A useful idiot. He had no idea what he'd stumbled into. And while I'd love to spend our time talking about my escapades, the clock is ticking. It may take the deputies a while to find us, but it won't take all night." He pouted. "Unfortunately. You are exquisite." His hand came around her throat, and he squeezed lightly. "I'm going to enjoy killing you." His licentious smile twisted her stomach. "After I've had my fun, of course."

His gaze dropped to the buttons on her uniform. He reached for the first one.

Laney knew she had seconds to act. Garrett's position pinning her arms gave him control of her upper body, but in his arrogance, he'd left her legs free. Drawing on her military combat training, she bent her knees sharply, pulling her legs up toward her chest. In the split second Garrett glanced down at the movement, she thrust her hips upward, creating just enough space to whip both legs around his neck. She locked her ankles behind his head, using her core muscles to tighten the grip.

Garrett's eyes widened in shock as she twisted her body violently to the side. The sudden shift in weight and leverage sent him toppling off her. His hands clawed at her legs, trying to break her hold, but she increased the pressure, using her thighs to cut off blood flow to his brain. He thrashed. She kept the hold, knowing that it would take time for him to lose consciousness.

And then his fingers wrapped around her injured ankle. White-hot pain exploded through her as he crushed the delicate bones with a bruising grip. She screamed and lost her hold on him.

Garrett scrambled away, coughing and choking, curse words eking past his lips.

Laney's own breathing was ragged as she struggled to her feet. She scooped up little Alli and turned to run when a hand locked on her uninjured leg. She spun with a solid round kick to the head, followed it with a groin shot, and then, for good measure, threw the dirt and rocks in her hands at his face.

Garrett fell back.

She ran.

Fiery agony burst from her ankle with every step. She feared it might be broken. Adrenaline kept her from succumbing to the pain. Her heart thundered as she ducked into the shelter of the trees. Roots and thick branches slowed her progress, but the thick foliage made her and Alli harder to find. Soon—far too soon—she heard Garrett's thundering footsteps behind her.

"I'm gonna kill you, Laney."

Terror rocketed through her. It sounded as if he was close. The weight of Alli's little body in her arms was a reminder of what could happen if she failed. Garrett was merciless. Laney didn't believe for a moment he wouldn't kill Alli. She was a witness.

And that's exactly why Garrett had targeted her. At least initially.

Until obsession took over.

Chest heaving, Laney plowed ahead. Pine needles smacked her face, and burrs tugged at her clothes. She tried to quiet her steps while still keeping up a quick pace, but it was hard.

Lightning burst overhead. The woods became as bright as day. Movement to the left caught Laney's attention. She whirled in time to see Garrett moving toward her. He held her gun. "Don't move, or I'll shoot you and the little girl."

She froze. Her mind whirled, trying to figure a way out of this, but every option put Alli at risk.

Suddenly the bushes next to her vibrated, and a blur of fur and motion whipped past Laney and leaped toward Garrett. He screamed. Laney turned to bolt when another form, this one much larger, burst out of the trees. Large hands grabbed Laney's shoulders. She began to resist when a voice said, "Take cover with Alli."

Her knees went weak with relief.

Jonah!

He released her, and she took shelter with little Alli behind a thick copse of trees. Garrett was still screaming. Fierce growls broke through the sound of the rain. Then Jonah ordered Garrett to shut up. The sound of his command, spoken in the quintessential grumpy Jonah way, sent tears spilling over her cheeks.

"Good girl, Scout. Now let go..." The growls grew louder, and Garrett hollered in pain.

"Release." Jonah huffed and then hollered. "Laney, call your dog off. She won't listen to me."

"Release, Scout! Come!"

Two seconds later, her lab bounced through the foliage to Laney's side. She cried tears of joy, unbidden, and wrapped an arm around Scout. "Good girl. Good girl." Scout licked her face and sniffed Alli, her tail wagging. "Yes, you found us. Good girl."

With extreme difficulty, Laney opened the pocket of her cargo pants and removed Scout's reward. The lab grabbed hold of the stuffed squirrel and made it squeak.

Tate appeared in front of Laney, concern etched on

his features. He crouched down. "Are you hurt?" He lightly touched Alli's back. She whimpered. "Alli?"

"We're okay. But Brett was shot. He might be dead, I don't know."

"We found him already. He's alive."

Thank God. Laney may have suspected Brett, but she believed he hadn't been working with Garrett. His eager-to-please attitude had landed him in danger, and he'd panicked. While running for his life, he'd gotten turned around and lost.

"Help Jonah secure Garrett." She didn't want the love of her life to get shot because he didn't have someone to cover him.

Tate gave a sharp nod and moved in the direction of Garrett's cursing and Jonah's growled commands.

"If you don't shut up, I'm gonna leave you here to bleed out." Jonah's tone was laced with barely controlled rage. "You're lucky I don't have Scout come back here and take another chunk out of you. Although from the bruises on your face, it looks like Laney gave you a run for your money too." Tate must've joined them because then Jonah said, "About time you showed up. You forget how to run?"

"I was busy making sure Ryker didn't bleed to death. He'll be fine, by the way."

"I know. He's too annoying to die."

There was a slight scuffle, and then Tate said, "I've got him. Go see to Laney. I think she's hurt but too stubborn to say so."

She waited with bated breath until a moment later,

Jonah appeared next to her. His expression was tender and worried as he placed a warm hand on her cheek. The feel of his touch ignited a firewall of emotion inside her. Fresh tears blurred her vision. "You're alive."

"So are you." He glanced down at little Alli. "You saved her."

"No, we saved her."

"EMS is on the way. Andy is tracking my phone. Where are you hurt?"

"It's nothing that won't heal." She reached up to take his hand. It was the worst timing, but Laney could not let another minute go without saying the words in her heart. "I love you, Jonah. I've loved you for ten years and been too scared to admit it. My mom and dad... well, it doesn't matter anymore. I don't want fear to hold me back. I want a life with you. Forever."

"I know." He leaned forward and brushed the sweetest kiss across her lips. "I knew it the moment you kissed me by the car." Jonah backed away and smiled. "You know I'm never going to let you live it down that it took several life-threatening events before you finally admitted that you loved me."

A laugh bubbled up. "Watch it, Foster. No one likes a know-it-all."

TWENTY-SEVEN

Six weeks later

Jonah straightened his green tie before settling his tan cowboy hat on his head. In half an hour, he was going to be marrying the woman of his dreams. He turned around to face Ryker. "What do you think?"

"You're still ugly."

Jonah snorted. "You're just mad because you're still stuck in that sling for another two weeks and it doesn't go with your suit."

Ryker had taken a bullet to his left arm during Alli's rescue. The impact had fractured bone, requiring surgery and weeks in a cast. Now, the doctors had cleared him for light movement, but he still had to wear the sling until his next evaluation. With rehab, they promised, he'd regain full strength and range of motion.

Thankfully, little Alli had also fully recovered. The

sedative Mitch had given her wore off with no lasting effects, and she remembered nothing of her ordeal. Her parents had sent a gift, along with Alli's handmade thank-you card, several weeks later. Laney kept the card on her bookcase in her office.

Brett Harrison also survived. As Laney concluded after the attack, his helpful attitude had landed him in a dangerous situation. He'd moved back home to Colorado while recovering from his gunshot wound, and decided to stay there permanently.

"Even with this stupid thing, I'm still better looking than you." Ryker shook his head and sighed. "You sure Laney wants to marry you? I mean, waking up next to your ugly mug every day would make me question my life choices."

"Stop it." Hannah lightly smacked her husband on the shoulder. Her blonde hair was put into an intricate updo, but several strands framed her face, which was glowing. Jonah was one of the few people that knew she was pregnant. Nearly two months. He was over-the-moon for his friends. They were going to make a formal announcement next month, once they passed the first trimester. She assessed Jonah with the scrutiny of a seasoned prosecutor. "You look perfect."

"Thank you, Hannah." He glanced at his other groomsman. "Tate, you ready?"

"Yep." He rose from the armchair he'd been resting in and grinned. "I just gotta ask. Do I get a prize for being the last man standing? It's weird being the only single guy in Company A."

"Oh, I have someone I can introduce you to," Hannah grinned. "Let's talk after the ceremony."

"Dude." Ryker shook his head. "You have no idea what you've just done."

Hannah laughed. "Don't scare him." She hooked an arm through Tate's. "I'll tell you more as we take our places. Come on."

They filed out of the room and Ryker paused, his hand on the knob. "Hey, Jonah, you coming?"

"I'll be right there. Just need one more minute."

"Got it."

Ryker left and the silence settled around Jonah. He removed a jewelry box from the pocket of his suit and opened it. The bracelet was silver, delicate, with a cross and the date of their wedding etched in it. He'd intended to give it to Laney after the ceremony but suddenly felt it couldn't wait.

Would she like it? He turned the bracelet in his fingers, remembering all those years he'd spent in doubt. That persistent feeling that somehow he wasn't quite enough. Not smart enough for his academic family. Not accomplished enough compared to his Olympic sister and doctor brother. And for years, not the right man for Laney.

But he'd been wrong. He was the right man for her.

And he was good enough. Had always been.

Laney taught him that.

He left the room and headed down the hall. The last few weeks had been a whirlwind as the case that'd started all of this came to a close.

Mitch Caldwell had died in the shootout and Garrett Wheeler would never see the outside of a prison cell. He'd made a deal with the prosecutor to plead guilty if they gave him life in prison instead of the death penalty. Capturing the killer hadn't stopped the victims' families from suffering the loss, but Jonah prayed it brought them some measure of peace. Especially since Garrett explained everything in his confession.

He'd become obsessed with Ava, and when she turned him down for a date, he grew angry. Vengeful. Seeing her with Tyler in the ice cream shop at the end of the summer was the final straw. Jealous and bitter, Garrett put his darkest thoughts into action. He murdered Lisa and Nolan as practice. Then Tyler and Ava for his own gratification.

Laney arriving on the scene hadn't been part of the plan. But it'd set in motion a chain of events.

At first, Garrett wanted to kill her because she was a witness.

Then he became obsessed with her. Saw her as the ultimate challenge.

And Mitch... well, Garrett discovered Mitch was back in town, living in the woods, and decided to "mentor" him. With the threat of blackmail and the promise of money, Garrett ordered Mitch to keep an eye on Laney when he couldn't. That progressed to convincing Mitch to attack Papa Earl and helping with the final attack.

Jonah stepped out of the visitor center and into the brilliant October sunshine. People mingled about near the chairs and gazebo that had been set up on the grassy lawn leading to the lake. For the first and only time, Piney Woods State Park was closed on a Saturday. As the new superintendent, Laney had mixed feelings about shutting the park down to the public, but Andy insisted. In the end, she relented, because it was the only way all of her rangers and staff could attend the event.

Jonah slipped around the side of the building and jogged a short distance away to the nearest cabin. He knocked on the door and Breanna opened it. Her eyes widened. "What are you doing here?"

"I need to see Laney."

Her gaze narrowed. "Are you going to do something stupid?"

He blinked, confused about her meaning and then scowled. "Do you take me for a complete idiot? I've loved her for years. You think I'm gonna break up with her on our wedding day? Not a chance."

Scout trotted to the door. She had a pretty green bow wrapped around her neck, and her fur gleamed with a fresh bathing and brushing. The lab would walk down the aisle with the ring bearer and flower girl. Jonah bent to pat the dog and then tried to peer around Breanna. He could hear the faint sound of Laney's laughter but couldn't see her. "Where's Laney?"

"No!" Breanna held up a finger and stepped outside, pulling the door closed behind her. "You can't see the bride in her wedding dress before the ceremony."

His heart pounded. She was in her wedding dress.

This was actually happening.

He still couldn't believe it.

"I need to see her." He showed Breanna the box in his hand. "I have a gift for her."

"I'll give it—"

"No." He yanked it away from her. "I want to give it to Laney. Tie a blindfold around my eyes before you let me in. That way I won't see her in the wedding dress, but I can still give her the gift."

Breanna huffed. "Stay here." She went back inside and appeared moments later with a slip of fabric. "Tie this around your face."

He tucked the box back in his pants pocket and then did as she instructed. Jonah sensed Breanna waving a hand in front of his face, but he couldn't see it. "You're being ridiculous," he growled. "I can't see anything, so can I finally talk to Laney now?"

Breanna escorted him inside and then called for Laney. "Your groom is being a royal pain. It's not too late to change your mind, you know."

"Never." Laney's voice was confident and then Jonah sensed she was in the room with him. A burst of laughter sputtered out of her. "What did you do to him?"

"He can't see you in your dress. You two have five minutes."

Jonah couldn't see it, but he sensed Breanna left the room. The chatter of women's laughter filtered in from the back of the cabin.

And then a whisper of air brushed across his skin before two delicate hands framed his face and brought him down for a sweet kiss. He basked in the love she so freely gave. That moment in the woods, when she told him she loved him, had been the catalyst, but since then, they'd shared their deepest worries and darkest fears. And it'd only made them fall more and more in love.

Wrapping an arm around her waist, he deepened the kiss. When it was over, Laney breathlessly said, "I'm not sure we're supposed to do that before the ceremony."

"The rule said I can't see you, not that I can't kiss you. Besides, you started it."

She laughed. "Yes, I did."

"I have something for you." He pulled the box from his pocket and extended it. Laney's fingers brushed against his as she took it, and his already galloping heart kicked up another notch.

She gasped. "It's beautiful."

"I intended to give it to you after the ceremony, but... I couldn't wait." He paused. "I need you to know, I will always choose you. When life gets bumpy, or when you're struggling, you can hold on to me. I'll be your rock. I'll hold steady and keep the faith."

"Oh, Jonah..." She rose and kissed him again, lightly and ever-so-soft. "I know that. You've been everything I've ever needed. Always. I was just too stubborn and too scared to admit it. Thank you for being my friend. For waiting for me to get myself together..." Her voice choked up. "Ugh, I can't cry or it'll ruin my makeup and Breanna will kill me. Or you."

He sucked in a deep breath. "I'm not scared of your sister."

"Well, you should be!" Breanna called out. "I know what your middle name is and I'll use it, Jonah."

His mouth dropped open. "You told her?"

"She saw it on the marriage license. It's not my fault," Laney hissed. She turned him and steered him toward the door. "Better get out before she publicizes it." Crisp air cooled his heated cheeks. Before Laney could close the door, he put a hand against the wood to stop her. "I love you, Laney."

"I love you too." She blessed him with another kiss. "Hurry. I can't wait to marry you, so let's get this show on the road."

"I'll meet you at the end of the aisle."

She laughed. "I'll be the one in the white dress."

ALSO BY LYNN SHANNON

Texas Ranger Heroes Series

Ranger Protection

Ranger Redemption

Ranger Courage

Ranger Faith

Ranger Honor

Ranger Justice

Ranger Integrity

Ranger Loyalty

Ranger Bravery

Ranger Purpose

Ranger Belief

Ranger Devotion

Triumph Over Adversity Series

Calculated Risk

Critical Error

Necessary Peril

Strategic Plan

Covert Mission

Tactical Force

Would you like to know when my next book is released? Or when my novels go on sale? It's easy. Subscribe to my newsletter at www.lynnshannon.com and all of the info will come straight to your inbox!

Reviews help readers find books. Please consider leaving a review at your favorite place of purchase or anywhere you discover new books. Thank you.